THE DRIFTING COWBOY

By

WILL JAMES

ILLUSTRATED BY THE AUTHOR

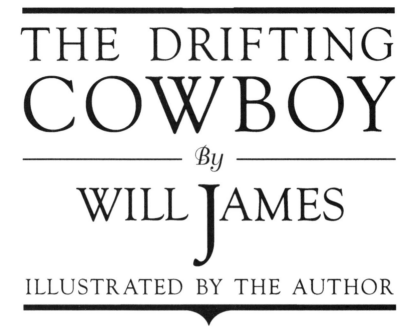

TUMBLEWEED · SERIES · D

MOUNTAIN PRESS PUBLISHING COMPANY
MISSOULA, MONTANA — 1995

Copyright © 1995
The Will James Art Company
Billings, Montana

Second Printing—September 1997

Library of Congress Cataloging-in-Publication Data

James, Will, 1892–1942.
  The drifting cowboy / by Will James ; illustrated by the author.
      p.   cm. — (Tumbleweed series)
  ISBN 0-87842-326-5 (pbk. : alk. paper) — ISBN 0-87842-325-7
(cloth : alk. paper)
    1. Cowboys—West (U.S.)—Social life and customs—Fiction.   2. Ranch life—
West (U.S.)—Fiction.   3. Western stories.
I. Title.   II. Series : James, Will, 1892–1942. Tumbleweed series.
PS3519.A5298D75   1995   95-4893
813'.52—dc20   CIP

Printed in the U.S.A. on acid-free recycled paper.

Mountain Press Publishing Company
P.O. Box 2399 • 1301 S. Third St. W.
Missoula, Montana 59806

PUBLISHER'S NOTE

Will James's books represent an American treasure. His writings and drawings introduced generations of captivated readers to the lifestyle and spirit of the American cowboy and the West. Following James's death in 1942, the reputation of this remarkable artist and writer languished, and nearly all of his twenty-four books went out of print. But in recent years, interest in James's work has surged, due in part to the publication of several biographies and film documentaries, public exhibitions of James's art, and the formation of the Will James Society.

Now, in conjunction with the Will James Art Company of Billings, Montana, Mountain Press Publishing Company is reprinting each of Will James's classic books in handsome cloth and paperback editions. The new editions contain all the original artwork and text, feature an attractive new design, and are printed on acid-free paper to ensure many years of reading pleasure. They will be republished under the name the Tumbleweed Series.

The republication of Will James's books would not have been possible without the help and support of the many fans of Will James. Because all James's books and artwork remain under copyright protection, the Will James Art Company has been instrumental in providing the necessary permissions and furnishing artwork. Special care has been taken to keep each volume in the Tumbleweed Series faithful to the original vision of Will James.

Mountain Press is pleased to make Will James's books available again. Read and enjoy!

The Will James Society was formed in 1992 as a nonprofit organization dedicated to preserving the memory and works of Will James. The society is one of the primary catalysts behind a growing interest in not only Will James and his work, but also the life and heritage of the working cowboy. For more information on the society, contact:

Will James Society, P.O. Box 8207, Roswell, NM 88202

BOOKS BY WILL JAMES

Cowboys North and South, 1924

The Drifting Cowboy, 1925

Smoky, the Cowhorse, 1926

Cow Country, 1927

Sand, 1929

Lone Cowboy, 1930

Sun Up, 1931

Big-Enough, 1931

Uncle Bill, 1932

All in the Day's Riding, 1933

The Three Mustangers, 1933

Home Ranch, 1935

Young Cowboy, 1935

In the Saddle with Uncle Bill, 1935

Scorpion, 1936

Cowboy in the Making, 1937

Flint Spears, 1938

Look-See with Uncle Bill, 1938

The Will James Cowboy Book, 1938

The Dark Horse, 1939

Horses I Have Known, 1940

My First Horse, 1940

The American Cowboy, 1942

Will James' Book of Cowboy Stories, 1951

PREFACE

THE DRIFTING COWBOY most likely says enough as it is without trying to describe what it's all about with a preface, but on account that a sort of introduction that way goes with every book, and regular the same as a good rope with a good saddle, I figger I ought to tell some of what the *drift* means in this perticular case of drifting.

In THE DRIFTING COWBOY, I don't mean that he's passing, and even though a quite a few have wrote on the passing of the cowboy *while going through on an observation car,* the cowboy has passed all he's going to for a spell. It's mighty sad and true that he has been crowded and that the land boosters have took some of that land away from him, but, as I've remarked in my first book, COWBOYS NORTH AND SOUTH, "there's still places where the cowboy can spread his loop without having it caught on a fence post."

There's still hundreds of miles of country where there's plenty of cattle and no fences, where the cowboy wears his boots out in the stirrup and *not* in irrigating ditches or shoveling hay. There's still outfits whose calf crops runs into thousands every year, many of them outfits have three round-up wagons out every season, with fifteen or twenty riders to each wagon, and a "remuda" of around two hundred saddle horses — So, figgering all, where does that cry "the cowboy has vanished" come in at?

In this book you'll find the cowboy still very much alive and all cowboy the same as ever as he drifts and hunts for new cow countries; the call from new ranges still makes him run in his saddle and pack horse and hit out; he often takes the train in drifting that way nowadays, and then again he might be seen hazing a gasoline-eating bronc acrost the valleys and mountains to some new stomping ground; but wherever or however he goes his saddle, ropes and chaps go with him, and always as he gets to the other end there's a string of ponies a-waiting for him.

As you turn the pages and follow the cowboy in his drifting, you'll see where he run acrost moving-picture camps and rode there a spell, you'll see him in a rodeo where he rides a few buckers or bulldogs a few steers while on the way. He drifts in the winter ahead of the blizzards and on through the summer, in the deserts, and where there's no shade, you'll meet the folks he meets and feel the breeze from the hoof of the same bronc he's saddling.

Some of the experiences described here I've felt and went through myself, and before my rope hand had ever felt a pen. There's some of the goings on that I've blamed on others, but that's the way it all happened, and I'm glad to feel, as I take the foot rope off this book and turns it loose, that the truth in it is not stretched, it can happen again.

Will James
III

CONTENTS

ILLUSTRATIONS

I'm lined up alongside the leading man, sized up one side and down the other and then I'm asked if I can ride.
~ page 39 ~

The director gives me the sign, and when my chance comes I sets down on the rein and pulls that horse over backwards.
~ page 41 ~

I shakes out my loop and spreads it right around that hombre's middle.
~ page 46 ~

How I catches me a wild horse as he comes in to water.
~ page 49 ~

Riding a bucking streak of greased lightning.
~ page 50 ~

We sure put 'er on wild, every horse had a fall and some two.
~ page 53 ~

I wondered how much a movie outfit would give for such a stampede as I was seeing.
~ page 61 ~

They'd sniff the air and at the first smell of coming moisture they'd line out acrost the hardpan flats and be on new range by the time the rain come.
~ page 75 ~

I didn't know none of the ponies, so I spreads my loop on the one that acted the spookiest.
~ page 81 ~

xiv

Even that big country round us looked kind of small and we're sure tearing it up.

It was no draw, that battle wasn't.

The next water hole was forty miles, and me being a stranger there I had to go on what I knowed of the desert to find that place.

Roping, wrestling, and branding big husky calves out on the big flats ain't as easy as it would be in some good corral.

She bellered like a steer when she found herself in the saddling shute and tried to climb over the high wall.

Tom made her think she couldn't buck a saddle blanket off.

But Tom managed to spread a good loop in steer roping.

The critter kept me up for a good airing.

I hear a snorting beller that sounds away off and I gets a glimpse of the roman-nosed, lantern-jawed head that was making it. . . . Old Angel Face was under me!

The lower bar of the corral was reached just in time.
~ page 165 ~

With the chance that pony had there, he'd killed most any of us, but with the Pilgrim he just picked him up and tossed him out of the way.
~ page 169 ~

As the Pilgrim stayed on with the outfit and watched the cowboys at work he found that they had no time to spend in saloons, he'd read of them shooting up town lights and making strangers dance, but he'd never as yet seen it done.
~ page 175 ~

The Pilgrim stayed behind, rode alongside of me, and talked all the way into camp.
~ page 177 ~

No rider had ever been able to make fun of him that way before.
~ page 197 ~

Dave was still in the game at thirty, which is when most of us are ready to quit the rough ones and start looking for the gentler kind.
~ page 202 ~

Some will go up in the air and let their feet go out from under 'em as they come down, and turn a somerset; sometimes two or three, before they stop rolling. A man ain't got much chance there.
~ page 205 ~

Their hoofs are not padded and a day of this would put ten years of the prize-fighting game in the kindergarten.
~ page 207 ~

Both hind feet shot out in a kick that seemed to make the saddle
horn and cantle touch.
~ page 209 ~

One squint at him and I felt right there that I wouldn't of knowed
him any better if we'd broke horses in the same corral for ten
years.
~ page 216 ~

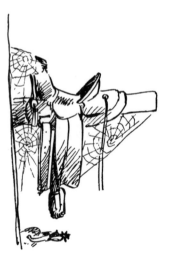

Chapter I

ONCE A COWBOY

I t was a mean fall, and on that account the round-up wagons was late with the works, and later getting in at the winter quarters. The cold raw winds of the early mornings wasn't at all agreeable to get up in, and I'd just about got so I could choke the cook when he hollered "Come and get it, you rannies, before I throw it out." We'd hear that holler long before daybreak, and sticking our heads out from under our tarps we'd greet the new day with a cuss word and a snort.

A wet snow would be falling and laying heavy on our beds, and feeling around between the tarp and blankets for socks we'd took off wet the night before, we'd find 'em froze stiff, but by the time they was pulled on and made to fit again and the boots over 'em, buckled on chaps and all what we could find to keep a feller warm, we wasn't holding no grudge against the cook, we just wanted a lot of that strong steaming hot coffee he'd just made and had waiting for us.

The bunch of us would amble up and around the fire like a pack of wolves, only there was no growling done; instead there'd be remarks passed around such as, "This is what makes a cowboy wonder what he done with his summer's wages." There'd be a whoop and a holler and a bucking cowhand would clatter up near top of the pots by the fire, "Make room, you waddies, Ise frizzed from my brisket both ways," and slapping his hands to his sides would edge in on the circle and grin at the bunch there before him.

The lids of the big dutch ovens was lifted, steaks, spuds and biscuits begin to disappear, but tracks was made most often toward the big coffeepot, and when the bait is washed down and the blood begins to circulate freer there was signs of daybreak, and rolling a cigarette we'd head for the muddy rope corral.

Our ropes would be stiff as cables, and it was hard to make a good catch. The particular pony you'd be wanting would most generally stick his head in the ground like a ostrich, and mixed in with about two hundred head of his kind and all a milling around steady, he'd be mighty hard to find again in case you missed your first throw.

Daylight being yet far off at that time, there's no way to identify any of the ten or twelve horses in your string only by the outline of their heads against the sky or by the white there may be on their foreheads. You threwed your rope but you couldn't see it sail and you didn't know you'd caught your horse till you felt the rope tighten up, and sometimes when you'd led out the horse you'd caught and got close to him it'd be another horse — the one you'd throwed the rope at had heard it coming and ducked.

Turning that horse back in the corral, you'd make another loop and try to get another sight of the horse you wanted; when you did, and the rope settled on him this time and let him out — if he didn't have to be drug out by a saddle horse — to your saddle, then's when the fun most generally did begin.

The snow and sleet and cold wind made the ponies, young or old, mighty sensitive to whatever touched 'em; they'd kick, and buck, and strike then, no matter how gentle some of 'em might of been when the nice weather was on. The cowboy, all bundled up on account of the cold, his feet wet and in the slippery mud the wet snow had made, finds it all a big drawback in handling himself when saddling and a flying hoof comes.

The shivering pony don't at all welcome the frozen and stiff saddle blanket, and it might have to be put on the second time; getting a short hold and hanging on to the hackamore rope the cowboy then picks up the saddle and eases it on that pony's back, and before that pony can buck it off, a reach is made for the cinch, the latigo put through the cinch ring and drawed up. If you work fast enough and know how, all that can be done, and you don't have to pick up your saddle and blanket out of the mud.

I've seen it on many a morning of that kind and you'd just about have your pony half in the humor of being good, when some roman-nosed lantern-jawed bronc would go to acting up, jerk away from a rider and try to kick him at the same time and go to bucking and a bawling, and with an empty saddle on his back, hackamore rope a dragging, would make a circle of the rope corral where all the boys would be saddling up.

The ponies led out and shivering under the cold saddle that put a hump in their backs would just be a waiting for such an excuse as that loose hunk of tornado to start 'em, and with a loud snort and a buck half of 'em would jerk away. The cowboy had no chance of holding 'em, for nine times out of ten that loose bronc would stampede past between him and the horse he was trying to hold, the hackamore rope would hook on the saddle of that bronc and it'd be jerked out of his hands.

Those folks who've seen rodeos from the grand stand most likely remember the last event of each day's doings; it's the wild-horse race, and maybe it'll be recollected how the track gets tore up by them wild ponies and how if one horse jerks loose he'll most likely make a few others break away. At them rodeos there's two men handling each horse, where with the round-up wagon on the range each man handles his horse alone.

And just picture for yourself the same happenings as you seen in the wild-horse race at the rodeo, only just add on to the picture that it's not near daylight, that instead of good sunshine and dry dirt to step on there's mud or gumbo six inches deep with snow and slush on top, the cowboy's cold wet feet, heavy wet chaps and coat that ties him down — a black cloudy sky, and with the cold raw wind comes a wet stinging snow to blind him.

That gives you a kind of an idea of how things may be along with the round-up wagon certain times of the year. Montana and Wyoming are real popular for rough weather as I've just described, and you can look for it there most every spring till late and sometimes in the fall starting early. I've seen that kind of weather last for two weeks at the time, clear up for one day and it was good to last for two weeks more.

It was no country for a tenderfoot to go playing cowboy in, besides the ponies of them countries wouldn't allow him to. It took nothing short of a long lean cowboy raised in the cow country to ride in it, and even though he'd cuss the weather, the country, and everything in general, there was a feeling back of them cuss words that brought a loving grin for the whole and the same that he was cussing.

Getting back to where a cowboy was saddling his horse and the stampeding bronc started the rumpus, I'll make it more natural and tell of how one little horse of that kind and on them cold mornings can just set the whole remuda saddled ponies and all to stampeding and leave near all the cowboys afoot.

Yessir, I remember well one cold drizzly morning that same fall, the wind was blowing at sixty per, the saddle blanket and saddle had to be put on at the same time or it'd blow out of the country. My horse was saddled and ready to top off, and pulling my hat down far as I could get it I proceeds to do that. I'm getting a handful of mane along with a short holt on my reins and am just easing up in the saddle. When I gets up about half ways I meets up with the shadow of another horse and trying to climb up on the other side of my horse. Me being only about a thousands pounds lighter than that shadow I'm knocked out of the way pronto, my horse goes down on part of me and that shadow keeps on a going as though there'd been nothing in its road.

That seemed to start things, and the wind that was blowing plenty strong already got a heap stronger, and all at once.

There was a racket of tearing canvas down by the chuck wagon and soon enough the big white tarpaulin that was covering that wagon breaks loose, comes a skipping over the brush, and then sails right up and amongst the two hundred saddle horses in the rope corral.

Them ponies sure didn't wait to see how and where it was going to light, they just picked up and flew, taking rope corral and everything right with 'em. A couple of the boys that was already mounted had to go too or else

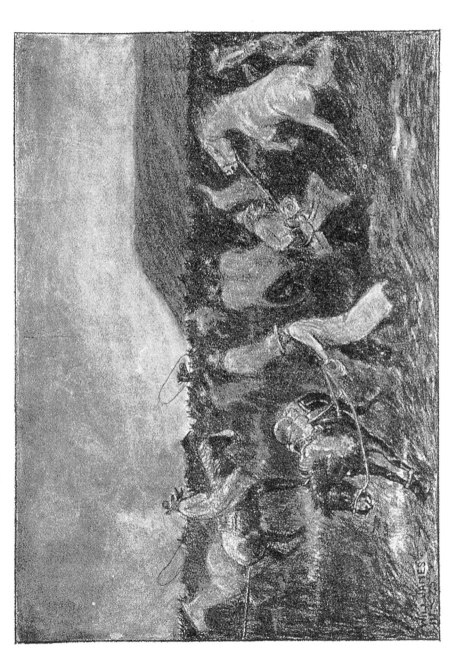

Yessir—I remember well one cold drizzly morning that same fall, the wind was blowing at sixty per, the saddle blanket and saddle had to be put on at the same time or it'd blow out of the country.

quit the pony they was riding, and they didn't have time to do that.

My horse being down for just the second he was knocked that way was up and gone, and I sure has to do some tall scrambling when the remuda broke out of the corral. I could near touch 'em as they went by and I'm drawing a long breath for the narrow escape I just had, when that same long breath is knocked out of me and I sails a ways, then lands in a heap. There must of been one horse I hadn't accounted for.

It's about daylight when I comes to enough to realize that I should pick myself up and get out of that brush I'd lit into. I'm gazing around kind of light-headed and wonders where everybody went, and finally, figgering that they'd be by the fire at the chuck wagon, makes my way that direction.

It's broad daylight by the time we hears the bells of the remuda coming back to the corral, some of the boys had put it up again while I was asleep in the brush, and the two riders what stampeded away when the remuda did was hazing the spooky ponies in again.

"Well, boys, we'll try it again," says the wagon boss as he dabs his rope on a big brown horse that was tearing around the corral.

Most of our ponies being already saddled it don't take us long to get lined out again. The boss is up

Me being only about a thousand pounds lighter than that shadow I'm knocked out of the way pronto.

on his horse, taking a silent count to see if any of his men are missing, while waiting for everybody to be on their horses and ready to follow him.

Our horses was all spooked up from that stampede, and when we started away from camp that morning it was a wild bunch for fair. I was trying to ease my pony into a lope without him breaking in two with me, and I just about had him out of the notion when there's a beller alongside of me, and I turns to see a bucking streak of horseflesh with a scratching cowboy atop of it headed straight my way.

It's a good thing I was ready to ride, 'cause my horse had been aching to act up from the start, and that example headed our way more than agreed with his spirits at that time. He went from there and started to wipe up the earth, and every time he'd hit the ground he'd beller, "I'll get you!"

At first I was satisfied to just be able to keep my saddle under me, but come a time when as my blood started circulating and getting warmed up on the subject that my spirits also answered the call and agreed with the goings on; then's when I begins to reefing him, and my own special war whoop sure tallied up with the bellering of that active valcano under me.

A glance to one side, and I notice that I'm not the only one who's putting up a ride, the rain and snow mixed kept me from seeing very far, but I could see far enough to tell that at least half the riders was busy on the same engagement that drawed my attention just then; one of the ponies had took a dislike for the cook and, tearing up everything as he went, was chasing him over pots and pans and finally under the wagon. The cowboy on top of that bronc was near losing his seat for laughing; he'd never seen the cook move that fast before.

We're out of camp a couple of miles before the usual rumpus quiets down, and stringing out on a high lope we all heads for a high point we don't see but know of, and some ten miles away. From that point the boss scatters the riders, and in pairs we branch out to circle and comb the country on the way back, running all the stock we see to the cutting grounds.

I'm riding along, trying to look through the steady-falling drizzle snow for stock; it seemed to me that I was born and raised under a slicker, on a wet saddle, riding a kinky bronc, going through slush and snow, and facing cold winds. It struck me as a coon's age since I seen good old sunshine, and for the first time I begins to wonder if a cow-puncher ain't just a plain locoed critter for sticking along with the round-up wagons as he does; it's most all knocks, and starting from his pony's hoofs on up to the long sharp horns of the ornery critters he's handling, along with the varieties the universe hands him in weather — twelve to sixteen hours in the saddle, three to four changes of horses a day, covering from seventy-five to a hundred miles, then there's one to two hours night guard to break the only few hours left to get a rest in.

The cowboy . . . was near losing his seat for laughing; he'd never seen the cook move that fast before.

We was moving camp for the last time that year, the next stop was the home ranch, and when we hooked up the cook's six-horse team and handed him the ribbons we all let out a war whoop that started the team that direction on a high lope. The cook wasn't holding 'em back any, and hitting it down a draw to the river bottoms the flying chuck wagon swayed out of sight.

Us riders was bringing in upwards of a thousand head of weaners and we didn't reach the big fields till late that day, when we finally got sight of the big cottonwoods near hiding the long log building of the home ranch; that, along with the high pole corrals, the sheds and stables, all looked mighty good to me again.

The stock turned loose, we all amble towards the corrals to unsaddle; I tries to lead my horse in the dry stable, but him being suspicious of anything with a roof on won't have it that way. "All right, little horse," I says to him, "if you're happier to be out like you've always been used to, I'm not going to try to spoil you," and pulling off my wet saddle I hangs it where it's dry for once. The pony trots off a ways, takes a good roll and, shaking himself afterwards, lets out a nicker and lopes out to join the remuda.

"Just like us punchers," I remarks, watching him; "don't know no better."

Over eight months had passed since I'd opened a door and set my feet on a wooden floor, and when I walks in the bunk house and at one end sees a big long table loaded down with hot victuals, and chairs to set on, I don't feel at all natural, but I'm mighty pleased at the change.

The Chink ranch cook is packing in more platters, and watching him making tracks around the table, looking comfortable and not at all worried of what it may be like outside, I'll be dag-gone if I didn't catch myself wishing I was in his warm moccasins.

The meal over with, I drags a bench over by one of the windows and, listening some to the boys what was going over the events that happened on the range that summer, I finds myself getting a lot of satisfaction from just a-setting there and looking out of the window; it was great to see bum weather and still feel warm and comfortable. I gets to stargazing and thinking, so that I plum forgets that there's twenty cowboys carrying on a lot of conversation in the same big room.

I'd just about come to the conclusion I was through punching cows when one of the boys digs me in the ribs and hollers, "Wake up, Bill! Time for second guard."

I did wake up, and them familiar words I'd heard every night for the last eight months struck me right where I lived; they was said as a joke, but right there and then I was sure I'd never want to stand no more of them midnight guards.

The work was over, and all but a few of the old hands was through. The superintendent gave us to understand as a parting word that any or all of us are welcome to stay at the ranch and make ourselves to home for the winter. "You can keep your private saddle horses in the barn and feed 'em hay. The cow foreman tells me," he goes on, "that you've all been mighty good cowboys, and I'm with him in hoping to see you all back with the outfit in time for the spring works."

A couple of days later finds me in town, my own top horse in the livery stable and me in a hotel. I makes a start to be anything but a cowboy by buying me a suit, a cap, shoes, and the whole outfit that goes with the town man. I then visits the barber and the bathtub, and in an hour I steps out thinking that outside my complexion and the way I walks I looks about the same as everybody else I see on the street.

I takes it easy for a few days, then gradually I tries to break myself to looking for a job where there's no ponies or bellering critters to contend with. I wanted an inside job where the howling blizzard wouldn't reach me and where I could have a roof over my head at night instead of a tarpaulin.

Time goes on, and it seems like my education is lacking considerable to qualify for the job I set out to get; you had to know as much as a schoolma'am to even get a look in. I made a circle every day and run in all the likely places I'd see. I tried grocery stores, hardware stores, and all kinds of stores, and when one day I runs across a sign in a candy-store window that says "Man wanted" I makes a high dive in the place before that sign disappears.

I'm stared at by a round-faced transparent-looking hombre back of a soft-drink counter. Two girls was a-sipping away on a straw and I had a hunch as I steps to one end of the counter that I'd butted in their conversation with the slick-haired gent.

Figgering on getting a lay of what I'd have to put up with on that kind of a job, I sticks around and orders something for the privilege. The confab is resumed again between the ladies and the clerk, and the more I listens to it the more I have doubts as to my ability to talk and still say nothing as them three are doing. I'm trying hard to get interested in the talk when in comes two more couples, there's sounds of "Hello, girls!" from something in pants, and answers of "Oh, hello, Dicky!" from the ladies, and that was enough for me, I steps out while they was still milling, and leaves 'em to their troubles. I didn't want to be particular, but that job was past me, and the wrong direction of what my ambitions pointed out.

I'm some leg weary as I makes my way back to the hotel that night, and going to my room I stretches out on the bed to rest up a little before I go out to eat. I have a feeling that all ain't well with me as I lays there thinking.

I don't want to think that I'm hankering to get back to the range, so blames it to the new ways of everything in general what comes with town life, and I tries to cheer myself up with the idea that I'll soon get used to it and in time like it.

"I got to like it," I says to myself, "and I'm going to stay with it till I do, 'cause I'm through with punching cows"; and getting up real determined I goes out to hunt a restaurant.

I'd been feeding up on ham and eggs and hamburger steak with onions ever since I hit town, and this night I thought I'd change my order to something more natural and what I'd been used to on the range.

"Bring me a rib steak about an inch thick," I says to the waiter, "Don't cook it too much, but just cripple the critter and drag 'er in."

I kept a waiting for the order to come, and about concluded he must of had to wait for the calf to grow some, when here he comes finally. I tackles the bait on the platter, and I was surprised to see a piece so much like beef, and still taste so different from any I'd ever et before. With a lot of work I managed to get away with half of it, and then my appetite, game as it was, had to leave me.

The waiter comes up a smiling as he sees I'm about through, and hands me the bill. "I don't want to spread it around," I says as I picks up the bill and goes to leave, "but between you and me, I'll bet you that steak you brought me has been cooked in the same grease that's been cooking my ham and eggs these last two weeks. I can taste 'em."

The weather had been good and stayed clear ever since I hit town, but as I walks out of the restaurant I notice a breeze had sprung up, and snow was starting to fall. I finds myself taking long whiffs of air that was sure refreshing after stepping out of that grub-smelling emporium.

Feeling rested up some, I faces the breeze for a walk and to no place in particular. I'm walking along, thinking as I go, when looking around to get the lay of my whereabouts I notices that right across the street from where I'm standing is the livery stable where I'd left my horse, and being that I'd only been over to see him once since I'd rode in, thinks I'd enjoy the feel of his hide once more.

The stable man walks in on us as we're getting real sociable, and with a "Howdy" asks if I may be looking for a job. "Man named Whitney, got a ranch down the river about fifty miles, asked me to look out for a man who'd want a job breaking horses on contract, and I thought maybe you'd be wanting to take it."

"Not me," I says, feeling tempted and refusing before considering. "I'm not riding any more, and I been looking for work in town."

"Did you try the Hay and Grain Market next block up the street?" he asks. "They was looking for a man some time back."

No, I hadn't tried it, but the next day bright and early I was on the grounds and looking for the major-domo of that outfit.

At noon that day I'd changed my suit, and putting on a suit of Mexican serge I went to work. My job was clerking, and on the retail end of the business, filling in orders and help load the stuff on the wagon of the customers.

And that night, when the place closed up and I walks to my hotel I felt a heap better than any time since I'd hit town. Of course I wasn't in love with the job, it was quite a change and mighty tame compared to punching cows, but then I figgered a feller had to allow some so's to get what he's after.

I gets along fine with everybody around, and it ain't long before I'm invited to different gatherings that's pulled off now and again. I gets acquainted more as I stays on, and comes a time when if feeling sort of lonesome I know where to go and spend my evenings.

I'd manage to stop in at the stable and say "Hello" to my gray horse most every night when the work was through, and with everything in general going smooth I thought it wasn't so bad.

There was times though when coming to my room I'd find myself staring at my chaps and boots with the spurs still on and where I'd put 'em in the corner. They got to drawing my attention so that I had to hide 'em in the closet where I couldn't see 'em, and then I thinks, "What about my horse and saddle? A town man don't have no need for anything like that."

But somehow I didn't want to think on that subject none at all right then, and I drops it, allowing that a feller can't break away from what all he's been raised with or at in too short a time.

That winter was a mean one, just as mean as the fall before I still remembered; the snow was piled up heavy on the hills around town and every once in a while there'd be another storm adding on a few inches. The sight of it and the cold winds a howling by on the streets kept me contented some, and it all helped break me in to the new ways of living I'd picked on.

I'd been on the job a month or so when I notice that my appetite begins to leave me. I changes eating places often, but they all seemed to have the same smell as you walked in, and there was times when I felt like taking the decorated platter and all outside and eating it there.

And what's more, my complexion was getting light, too light.

January and February had come and went, the cold spell broke up some, and then March set in wild and wicked. I'm still at my job at the Feed Market and my wages being raised once along with promises of another raise soon, proves that I'm doing well. What's more, my time had been took up considerable on account of me meeting up with a young lady what put my gray horse a far second in my thoughts, and when I'd walk past the stable I'd most generally be in too big a hurry to stop and see him. One day the stable man stops me as I'm hurrying by and tells me that he has a chance to sell that little horse for me for a hundred dollars.

That was a call for a show-down to myself, and of a sudden I realized that parting with that horse I was parting with the big open range I'd been born and raised into. I studies it over for quite a spell and finds the more I thinks the more my heart lays the ways of where that horse can take me, and my mind all a milling I can't decide.

I walks away, telling the stable man I'd let him know later.

I does a lot of comparing between the range and the town, and finds that both has qualities and drawbacks, only in town it was easier living, maybe too easy, but I figgered that here was more of a future.

Just the other day I was told by the main owner at the market that they was figgering on quitting the business and retiring, and that there'd be a good opportunity for a serious-thinking man like myself to grab. It was suggested that I could let my wages ride and buy shares with 'em as I worked till there'd come a time as I kept at it when I'd find myself part owner of a good business and a steady income.

That night I went to see the young lady, who by this time had a lot to say as to my actions. I didn't let her know what was going on in my think tank, 'cause I wanted to fight it out by myself; besides I'd come to conclusions, and long before I left her to go back to my hotel.

The next morning I stops by and tells the stable man that if he can get a hundred dollars for that little horse of mine, to take it. But it hit me pretty hard and I didn't go by the stable any more after that, not for a long time.

April come, and with the warm weather that came with it the snow started to melting, the streets was muddy, and the gutters was running full; it was spring, and even with all the resolutions I'd made, I didn't feel any too strong right then.

I was afraid to give my imagination full swing and think of the home ranch on the Big Dry; I knew the boys that came back for the spring works would be out on the horse round-up and getting ready to pull out with the wagons.

Each cowboy would be topping off his string about now, the bronc peeler would be picking out a bunch of green colts from the stock horses and start in breaking, the cook would be a cleaning up the chuck box on the back end of that wagon, and the cow foreman, glancing often on the road that leads from town to the ranch, would be looking for any of the missing cowboys what was with him the year before.

I found it mighty hard to walk away from that spring sunshine into the building where I was working. There was orders on the desk waiting for me to fill, and picking 'em up I walks among high walls of grain and baled hay.

Everybody I'd see would remark how great it was outside in the spring air, and rubbing their hands would get to work at the desk and typewriter, and forget all about it the minute they set down.

I felt sorry for 'em in a way, 'cause it struck me as though they'd never had a chance to really appreciate springtime — or was it that their years in captivity that way had learnt 'em better than to hanker for such?

Anyway, I sure didn't seem to be able to dodge how I felt. My girl and everybody else noticed it, and even though I'd try to laugh it off I'd soon find myself picturing little white-faced calves scattered out either playing or sunning themselves while their mammies was feeding on the new green grass.

I could near feel the slick shiny hide of the ponies after their long winter hair had just fell off. And dag-gone it it was getting the best of me.

I'd catch myself sneaking glances at the green hills around the town and feeling as though I had no right to. And once in a while in the evening as I'd be walking to my room and I'd hear a meadow lark a-singing way off in the distance, I'd look at the buildings, the sidewalks and streets as though they was a scab on this earth. I wanted my horse under me and lope out away from it.

I'd done a heap of reasoning with myself, and kept a pointing out all the whys I should forget the range and get used to the town, and I'd pretty near give in as long as I was in my room and couldn't feel the breeze, but once outside again and a meadow lark sang out, my heart would choke out all what the town offered and leave breath only for the blue ridges and the big stretches that layed past 'em.

Then came a day when my hide got too thick to feel the reasoning spur I was giving it. Something way deep inside of me took charge of things and I finds myself making tracks towards the stable.

I sneaks in, and I had to rub my eyes considerable to make sure that there in the same box stall was my little gray horse, fat as a seal and a snorting like a steam engine.

"Dag-gone your hide!" I says, and I makes a grab for him, he's pawing the air snorting and a rearing, but I'm hanging on to his neck with a death grip and hands him all the pet cuss words I can think of.

The stable man runs up to see what's making all the rumpus, and his expressions tell me plain he thinks I'm drunk and celebrating. I was drunk all right, but not on the same stuff that's handed over the bar.

"Sorry I couldn't sell him for you," I hear him say as I let go of my horse and walks up to him, "but the fellow what wanted him came over one day to try the horse out and the little son of a gun throwed him off as fast as he'd get on; he brought another feller over the next day and the same thing happened. Too bad he acts that way," he goes on, "'cause he's a right pretty horse."

"You're dag-gone right he's a pretty horse" I says; "the prettiest horse I ever seen."

I'm hanging on to his neck with a death grip and
hands him all the pet cuss words I can think of.

*He brought another feller over the next day
and the same thing happened.*

It's three days later when I gets sight of the Triangle F main herd, then the remuda, and down in a creek bottom by a bunch of willows is the chuck wagon.

There's war whoops from the bunch as I lopes into sight, and the wagon boss comes up to meet me. "I knowed you'd be back, Bill," he says, smiling, "and I got your string of ponies a waiting for you, twelve of 'em."

And on guard that night, riding around the bedded herd, I was singing a song of the trail herd, happy again, and just a cowboy.

Chapter II

FILLING IN THE CRACKS

A bronc kicking me in the jaw is what started me to looking for a altogether different country than what I'd been used to, and away to where there's more folks and specialists, jawbone specialists mostly.

A kick is something you can't always dodge, wether it be from a human or a horse. And this bronc maybe meant no harm and was only acting according to his instinct towards the human, but anyway I underestimated his reach by an inch, with the result that the boys had to straighten me up and lay me in the shade of the chuck wagon to recuperate some.

A few days of shade, soft grub, and pain and I'm trying to think of some place to go where I can get my grinders tended to, when one of the boys suggests Los Angeles, remarking that he knows one *hombre* on the outskirts of that town who could sure fix me up good as new.

That sounded kind of promising; — besides I wanted to see Los Angeles. I thinks it over careful for a day or so and finally decides to head that direction. I asks for my wages with a few months in advance throwed in, sells my two saddle horses that was laying around at the home ranch, and with the few hundred dollars in my pocket I hits for the nearest railroad and buys me a yard of ticket for Los Angeles, two thousand miles to the south and west.

I'm getting good and tired of soft grub by the time I see the smoke of that town and I don't lose no time hunting up the specialist and putting him to work. He tells me after looking things over that it'd take a couple of months to fix me up; and when I steps out and looks around, I wonders what I'm going to do with all the spare time I'll have.

I runs across a saddle shop where I fingers saddle leather, looks over the silver-mounted bits and spurs and wishing all the time I was a millionaire; then sashays out the beach where they all tell me it's the place to go to have a good time and see the sights; but it didn't interest me none and after going over there every day, covering twenty miles of beach country and not seeing what I calls a good time or sights, the time and days are dragging along mighty slow.

I'm there about a week and getting awful homesick for the range, when, roaming around one day I gets the real surprise of my life and runs across a altogether different atmosphere, the likes of which sure set me blinking and staring. — A cow town it was; and right here at the edge of the tall stone and brick buildings of Los Angeles, instead of automobiles was buckboards, ponies was tied here and there, and cowboys, the same I'd seen up in the Montana town I'd just left was sticking around and taking it easy.

It was sure good for sore eyes, and I even forgot about my bum jaw. I parades around and takes in the best sights I'd seen for quite a spell, and when I turns a corner and comes face to face with two real pretty cowgirls I come near giving myself away and saying, "Aw."

I goes on a little further and doubles back on my tracks, for I sure didn't want to lose the whereabouts of that spot that really belonged up in Montana or Wyoming somewhere. I passes corrals full of horses and longhorned Mexico cattle. There's stage coaches and prairie schooners by the stables and in the shade of them was the old-time Cherokee and Sioux bucks and squaws all in war feathers and paint.

Daggone it, the whole kaboodle sure looked mighty good to me, and when a little later I struts by the saloon and hears a argument between a "dally" and a "tie" man I begins to feel right at home. One of the boys arguing has his back turned, and that back looked familiar to me and his voice I'd heard before somewhere. The argument goes on good-natured and I'm listening, at the same time trying to place just where I'd seen that back and heard that voice. It all comes to me of a sudden just as he moves his arm to illustrate his point in the argument, for I'd often seen that arm in the same motion at throwing the rope.

"What the hell do you know about a tied rope, Sam?" I asks, breaking in on the confab. I'm ginning at him when he turns around to see who's making all the noise and I see he don't recognize me in my store clothes; I waits a while then

I says, "Remember the Z-X and Slivery Bill?" That was enough, and Sam Long just busts hisself getting down off the saloon steps over to me. I missed my appointment with the Doc that day.

I finds while I'm getting introduced to the boys around that this little cow territory I'd run into was called Edendale, that it was the place where all the moving picture producers got their men when they wanted real cowboys for Western pictures, there was studios right close and Hollywood or Universal City was a short ride on horseback. The boys was kept busy most of the time and when they wasn't, they'd be practicing up on bronc riding, steer riding, steer roping, or bull-dogging and getting in shape to compete in rodeos wherever they was held; they was professional contest hands and mighty hard to beat.

There was plenty of stock to practice on, and amongst that stock was anything a picture director could call for and any amount from the meanest bucking horse down to the bob-tailed roach-maned english thoroughbred; all was used in pictures along with the boys and none had a chance to get rusty.

I'm told a lot about the inside of the picture game and I'm all interested. Then Sam suggests that I join the crowd: "you just got to" he says "and with that face you got there's all the chances of you being a leading man, if any time a good horse-thief character is wanted."

Anyway I sticks around for a spell and one day comes news that a big "western" is going to be filmed, — they'd

And afterwards us boys was called on
to do our bit on bucking horses.

need a hundred riders and most all the bucking stock and steers around Edendale besides a hundred saddle horses. Before I know it, Sam has my name on the list and I'm one of the extras at five dollars a day for a month steady — you can bet your boots I didn't kick, for I couldn't of found a better way to make my expenses; besides being with my own breed of folks was a plenty to keep me agreeable.

"Six-guns and Ropes" was the starting name of this picture where I introduces myself to the screen. It was supposed to've been of the days when most everybody wore red flannel shirts and was overweighed about twenty pounds with guns and ammunition. Us boys had to mash down the crown of our hats to make 'em match up with them times and a few was picked out of the crowd to wear full beards, — about that time Sam and I was missing and didn't show up till everything was safe.

A "Fiesta" was pulled off, and afterwards us boys was called on to do our bit on bucking horses, steer roping and the like. There was no rehearsing on our stuff and the director was tickled the way we went at it.

Then, I gets a vision of the leading man strutting in the arena. I'd seen him on the screen many a time and thinks to myself "here's where I'm going to see some bronc riding that'll make our efforts look sick." The director is walking along with him and heads over to us fellers setting by the chute; they both give us the once over, and I'm wondering what for when that same director crooks his finger at me asking me to come over.

I'm lined up alongside the leading man, sized up one side and down the other and then I'm asked if I can ride — I'm thinking maybe I was picked on to show the world what a bum cowboy I am compared to that leading man and I'm not hankering for such, so I says, "I can ride, *some*."

I'm lined up alongside the leading man, sized up one side and down the other and then I'm asked if I can ride.

Then the director comes back at me with, "aren't you the fellow that rode that Graeagle bucking horse a while ago?" and I says "yes." — "Well then you'll do fine," he says walking away and telling me to come along.

I tags along doing some tall wondering till we get to a big car on the edge of the grounds, and there I'm told I'd get five dollars extra if I'd ride another bucking horse like I did Graeagle and wear the leading man's clothes, "and if you can get your horse in front of the camera and pull him over backwards when I give you the sign, I'll give you twenty dollars more," says the director.

I begins to see light as I accept the terms, I'm all dolled up and prances out following the director to where a big brown horse is snubbed and blind-folded, the camera is off a ways and ready for action and I'm to start from there, saddling the brown, mounting him and do my bestest to follow the instructions.

I'm warned not to let the camera see my face any more than I can help and I keeps that in mind as I pulls off the blind, let out a war whoop and begins fanning said bronc.

The show is on, the camera is grinding, the bronc is a bawling, tearing up the earth and scattering himself all over creation and universe; I'm fanning him, and every time the horse faces the camera I covers my face with my hat, at the same time making it look natural as I can and in fanning motion.

Then the director gives me the sign and when my chance comes I sets down on the rein and pulls that horse over backwards as pretty as you please. Down we come, all in a heap but I took care to see that I was in the clear and when the bronc starts up again I'm right in middle of him, and finishes the grandstand ride in good style.

*The director gives me the sign, and when my chance comes
I sets down on the rein and pulls that horse over backwards.*

The director acts mighty pleased the way I done it and tells me that I couldn't done better if I tried, which after thinking it over means a whole lot. Then the leading man steps up, does a heap of congratulating and wants to give me an extra twenty dollar bill for the good work, as he put it.

But some way I'm disappointed in him, and I tells my feelings to Sam. "From seeing him in the picture," I says "I thought this hombre was a top 'ranahan,' a he wolf on a horse, and it sure gets me deep to learn that he couldn't ride in a box car with both doors shut, and couldn't throw a rope in the ocean, if he was in the middle of it in a rowboat. He admits that himself and still, they keep on fooling the people to thinking he's a real cowboy."

"Now wait a minute," Sam says, "you're pawing at the hackamore without knowing what's hurting you. Stick around for a spell and I can talk to you better about it, but for the time being let me tell you that this leading man is getting a thousand to your thirty dollars a week, that if he was to get hurt the whole company would be held up till he recuperated, the picture would be delayed, his wages would have to be paid along with others, and the bed rock of it is that his contract reads where he's not to take any chances on anything dangerous and where he can be 'doubled.'

"What's more," Sam goes on, "he's got talent, he can act and people want to see him for that most. They're not worried much wether he's a real cowboy or not so long as he can roll his eyes right and at the right time. Put yourself in his place and try to act, how far would you get and how much would you be drawing from the company? — your expression is just the same wether you're eating a plate of 'frijoles' or riding a bronc; fact is you aint got no such thing as expression and far as you'd get is what you done to-day; or as I said before, if a good horse-thief character is wanted you might shine there."

"Hold on there, Sam," I manages to squeeze in between breaths, "I think I understand, and before we go any further on this subject I'll wait and do as you say, I'll stick around for a spell and when I get enough information to start another argument I'll get you over to one side and have it out with you."

I walks off, rolls me a cigarette and thinks it all over. No doubt Sam was right, but to me it didn't strike me right, that one man should do all the dangerous work and have the other feller get all the credit for it, when all he did was congratulate after all was over — of course nobody cares about the credit much, but there was something about it that hit the wrong spot, with me.

We're working along up in the hills, taking the part of outlaws one day and being a posse chasing them same outlaws the next day. We're taking some mighty steep hills and coming down off 'em hell bent for election and the leading man is *trying* to ride with us, but he finally has to be doubled again for the reason that he couldn't stay in the lead where he was supposed to be. Instead of that he'd be so far back that it'd take him a half hour to catch up. He'd rode in the cavalry and at chasing foxes but this was different. A heap different.

A few days later the director asks me if I wouldn't double for his leading man again, and jump my horse over a twenty foot cliff they'd located for the picture; *that* set me to thinking for quite a while before answering, but I finally agrees.

It had to be done twice being we didn't fall good enough the first time, but I got twice my price and outside of a sprained ankle and a skinned elbow felt pretty good.

I layed around camp for a few days rubbing my ankle with liniment and Sam was taking every chance he had to come over and pester the life out of me; like one time I see him riding up packing a grin a mile long, I knew right away he had something good to spring on me, and I got ready. "Now Bill," he begins, "do you see the difference between a man what works with both his feet and hands, and another man what works with his head?" — He turns his horse and tries to get away, but one of my boots caught up with him and left him serious.

"Come on, Sam," I hollered at him, "spring another one."

Then one morning, the director walks up to me and asks when I'll be able to ride again, remarking that he'd like to give me a small part in the picture and he begins to explain what I'm to do, I'm to be one of the boys what's to help the hero round up that bunch of desperate outlaws he's after, we're to do most everything but rescue the heroine, and as the director tells me it's just something extra and of his own thinking to give the picture more punch.

"I'd like to have you do a little bulldogging too," he says, "and maybe some more wild horse stuff, if we can chip it in along the story."

I finds that Sam is in the outlaw gang we're supposed to corral, and something hatches up in my mind that's too good to leave go, wether it makes a hit or I get fired off the lot for it, anyway, I'm not worried.

We're chasing Sam and his crowd of horse thieves all over the country, over hills and across washouts for a whole day, and when the last close-up of the chase comes along I begins to get ready. So far, we'd been doing nothing but chasing and swapping shots and when this time the director hollers "get ready — cam-e-r-a" instead of getting out my six-gun as I was expected to do I uncoils my rope, builds me a loop and away I go.

Sam is way ahead with his bunch of desperadoes, but in this last shot we're supposed to corner 'em, and we sure do. I passes 'em all like they was standing still and heads for one certain party who's supposed to be the only one getting away (according to the story) but I'm out to spoil his plans. I shakes out my loop and

*I shakes out my loop and spreads it right
around that hombre's middle.*

spreads it right around that hombre's middle, jerks him off his horse right where the camera can get it all and at close range.

Sam is real surprised, — I'm off my horse before he can come out of it, and moving picture style I lets him stare into the business end of my six-shooter. He's staring alright, and wondering what's up, but I keep up my acting, and real sarcastic, at the same time having a hard time to keep from laughing I tells him that *he sure makes a dandy character of a horse thief.*

About that time, the director who's doing a heap of wondering and staring himself had let the camera grind, and when he comes to himself orders the camera man to "cut."

I'm feeling kinda foolish and expects to get fired right there. Then I sneaks a peek at the director again who's looking at the ground like he was going to bore a hole through it, and somehow by the way he's thinking and trying to grin a little I have hopes.

In the meantime Sam'd shook off the dust he'd gathered, turns on me real vicious and asks what the hell I'm trying to pull off. "Nothing much, you jughead," I answers, "just trying to even scores on the bright remarks you passed off and on. I was real easy with you," I goes on, "I could of drug you all over these hills if I wanted to."

Sam thinks it over for a spell, and pretty soon he begins to see light and says, "all right, Bill, we're even now and let's stay that way."

The director picks up the magaphone and hollers "get ready folks, we'll take this last scene over again, and everybody do as directed *please*"; — that last was meant for me I know, and when I looks over his way to make sure, he gives me the wink like as to say he'd forgive me this time.

I'd been over to see the dentist pretty regular, my appointments was changed for evenings, and I was getting in fair shape to be able to laugh again without hiding my face with my fist. I was glad of it cause I didn't want to get to work on the little part the director gave and run chances of showing a toothless grin.

I played some pony express, a few close-ups by my lonesome, and others with the leading man showing where I'm delivering some important papers; then again where my horse breaks a leg in a badger hole and how I catches me a wild horse as he comes in to water, saddles him when he's down, gets on and proceeds, riding a bucking streak of greased lightning and delivers the important message at the other end.

I does the bulldogging stunt and saves the fair heroine from an awful death; but in this one I'm wearing the leading man's clothes and I'm congratulated again, but I wasn't the only one to be congratulated and wearing such clothes as the leading man's, there was two other boys (ham actors) called on to double for him: one to rescue a dummy supposed to be the heroine and come down on the outside of a twenty story building; — I thought it was

How I catches me a wild horse as he comes in to water.

Riding a bucking streak of greased lightning.

a pretty ticklish job myself, and I couldn't blame the leading man much if he was glad to be out of it. The other boy done a high dive, about fifty feet into the ocean to rescue that very same heroine once more, and I didn't want that job either, — diving or coming down off tall buildings was plum out of my line, and I didn't hanker for it, none at all.

Well, the picture went on, we corralled all the outlaws, Sam with 'em and put 'em all in jail, — the heroine was rescued once again out of the clutches of a villian and she decides to marry the hero.

Another big fiesta was pulled off and everybody was having a great time, and celebrating on the good work of ridding the country of desperadoes (who all was enjoying themselves right with us and dressed for the occasion as we were), the leading man and lady was married right there and that ended the stirring photoplay of "Six-guns and Ropes."

It took five weeks to grind that picture, and on the last day when everything is being took off the sets and put away in the "prop" rooms, the director gets me over to one side and tells me about the time I roped Sam and drug him off his horse. "That was the best piece of work I ever looked at" he says "and when I saw it in the projection room, I found it so much better than plain acting that I'm going to try and make it fit in the story somehow, the expression on Sam was great, he wasn't expecting that and he sure registered surprise without trying, which makes it good." And you he says "sure looked as though you meant it."

He winds up by telling me to be sure and be around when he starts on his next western.

The rainy season was with us and the cameras wasn't being used much, I'd been laying around for near three weeks when the weather shows signs of clearing and I gets some work from another company. Sam and me and a few other cowboys went and rode for a few days in a steeple chase as jockeys, and we sure put 'er on wild, every horse had a fall and some two; four riders went to the hospital for a while, and one of 'em doubling for the leading lady who according to the story was supposed to win the race got the worst of it and stepped on a whole lot, but that was in the story and that horse was supposed to fall; he only "pulled" and throwed him when he was told to. It was exciting alright and the leading lady thought it was grand, till she found out how badly hurt the rider was.

But none of the boys kicked, they took their own chances and accepted the consequences the way they was dealt, and the rest of us boys what was still altogether kept on riding the postage stamp saddles, and putting our horses over the hurdles and water holes the same as before till our work was thru.

It started to cloud up and rain again, and kept up a steady fog and drizzle day after day, the movie folks stayed inside with the camera, and us boys hung around the stables and tried to pass the time away the best we could. We was mighty glad when the weather cleared up again

We sure put 'er on wild, every horse had a fall and some two.

and most tickled to death when we hears that one of the big companies was going to start in on a seven reeler western drama.

We all hung around the phone at the stable like a bunch of ants, waiting to hear the good words of "get ready" — finally it comes. They'd need a hundred riders to make up as the early days man on horseback, such as the injun fighter and scout in buckskin, trappers and spaniards, and two hundred injuns with teepees, ponies and squaws all in full war paint. They'd also want twenty prairie schooners all fixed up with ox teams, some with mules or horses, along with about a hundred head of loose stock, mostly cattle: — could we fix 'em up? "We sure can" Curly Jones answers "and if you need any hogs or geese and chickens and goats and burros and —," but about that time the receiver at the other end was hung up and Curly turns around to tell us "get ready boys, and tell the other fellers down the line to sashay right over here if they want to get work on this one, it'll mean about six weeks and maybe more."

Well, we're ready in no time and stringing out on location a few miles out in the hills, it sure made some outfit, and you wouldn't think the way all of us boys was mixing with the injuns and kidding along that soon there'd be a terrible fight between them reds and us whites, — well, there was and we was all massacreed, all but a little orphant what was hid in the blankets that the fire didn't get, — *and there was the story.*

There was a heap of acting in that picture, a few running fights and the burning of a frontier town. Us boys was used mostly to fill in the cracks in the background, making things look natural, outside of that we didn't figger much.

It got monotonous, that is for me anyway cause I was one of the bunch what was entirely willing to let the other feller "hog the foreground."

We'd been at it near six weeks and the picture wasn't over half done, the rain and fog kept a driving us in every once in a while and there was a lot of time lost on that account. And every time we'd come out again I'd keep a noticing how nice and green the country was getting to be, that old phony, petrified looking grass that covered the hills when I first come had disappeared and instead of it there was great long stems of that green new grass.

But it all looked too pretty to suit me, and gave me the feeling that here was a country the likes of which you'd find after crossing the Great Divide and your boots was pulled off for the last time.

April come along, and I was finding myself doing a lot of dreaming, picturing in my mind just how that country to the north and east would look at this perticular time, I could kind of see the snow most all melted away leaving the big patches of green where little white faced calves are sunning themselves and everything all quiet. The boys back there would be getting ready for the spring round up soon and running in the "remudas."

Daggone it, I was getting homesick, and when one day a letter is handed out to me and I reads the few words it said, I know right away I'm going and "poco tiempo."

A little bunch of green buffalo grass was in the letter and that alone was enough, the few words only made me act all the quicker saying "come and get it or I'll throw it out: (meaning the cook's holler to grub pile) and, "we'll be pulling out soon for the spring works, will you be with us?" It was signed by Tom Rawlins, cow foreman of the "circle dot."

Would I be with 'em? — I sure would, or else break my neck trying. I showed the letter to Sam, and it pretty near got him too, for awhile, but he'd been in the picture game too long to quit so sudden and after thinking it over decides to stick it out for a spell longer, "I don't think I'd be much good on the range any more" he tells me "but I hate to see you go, Bill, cause you're the only one around here I like to argue with; — anyway, I think you'll be back again soon and I'll try to stick around till you are."

"All right, Sam," I says, "but don't stand on your head all that time, will you?"

My bridle teeth and grinders being all fixed up and good as new, I feel pretty good as I pack up and grabs the first train going out, and the next morning when I wakes up, goes out to the rear of the train and sees sage brush again, I feell considerable better. The sight of the cottonwoods and real he-mountains on the way sure made me perk up my ears and take a long breath, and the thought of just living and knowing just where I was headed was a plenty to keep me more than contented.

As the train traveled on I'd find myself wondering how them broncs I'd started to break last spring was going to pan out this year, how many of the boys I know will be back to join the outfit and how the stock pulled thru the winter.

I figgered it kind of queer that it didn't bother me to leave the movie game and the good folks I'd met there, but I layed it to the fact I wasn't cut out to be a actor anyway. I'd found it easier living there in a way and more fun than we'd have on the range, but I didn't get no satisfaction out of that and got to hankering for something more real and what I was raised to doing.

I wanted to stand night-guard again with the snow or sleet flying by, and hear the range critter's beller without the camera being near, — I wanted the *real thing*.

And the real thing was right there, seemed like waiting for me when the train stopped at Malta, it was the old "circle dot" chuckwagon and the cook who'd just drove in to get a few months' supply of grub to carry the outfit through the round up. The first thing struck my eye was the brand, made with a "running iron" and burned deep on the fresh rawhide covering the side jockey box of the wagon.

The sight of the whole layout brought a lot of things back to memory, for I'd et many a meal alongside of it in all kinds of weather and with many different riders. I remembered the time I layed in the shade of that same old wagon for a good two months with a busted leg, and how I'd pester the cook to make us some "son-of-a-gun-in-the-sack" for a change.

Them happenings was all the real thing, no acting about it, and it didn't get under your hide like the other did in time.

It seemed to me like I'd been gone four years instead of months and when I run across some of the boys and Tom Rawlins a little while later, I think the way I acted made 'em get the hunch that I'd been abused while down in Los Angeles.

I tells 'em of me working in the movies, careful not to mention Sam, being I didn't know how he stood with the sheriff here. They was surprised that a common

looking hombre like me could get in the movies at all
(I was too at first but I didn't say so), and when they
ask me what all I done in the line of acting. I says
"nothing much, just stood out in the background and
filled in the cracks."

My string of company horses was turned over to
me, twelve head of 'em; Tom tells me they hadn't been
rode since I left and they sure looked it, all fat as butter
and full of kinks, and I saw where I'd sure have to ride
close to my saddle if I didn't want to walk. But I got
along all right, this was something I was raised at doing
and knowed how to take.

I stayed with the outfit all thru the spring and
summer. We was done with the fall round-up, put the
weaners under fence and on the way to the shipping
point with some of the beef herd, three thousand head
of fine big three year olds; — we are taking 'em slow
and letting 'em graze as they go.

The fourth night out, and about half way to the
railroad a double guard was put on, six men instead of
three, and by all indications in the sky which was sure
threatening I had a hunch that all of us six riders would
have our hands full long before the time for the next
"relief."

And my hunch was right, only it come quicker than
I expected. The stiff wind, rain, lightning, and thunder
didn't follow one another as it usually does in such
cases, they all came together fast and furious and trying
to beat one another, seemed like.

And the cattle didn't fool with preliminaries of milling around before starting out; they all got up at once and went from there, every single critter as quick as the other and moving the same as one, three thousand head of 'em and stampeding down the draw, — not a beller was heard and we all saw where *we sure had to ride.*

Our six-shooters was a smoking and tearing up the earth in front of the leaders trying to scare 'em into turning and milling and about the time we'd get some control of 'em a few streaks of chained lightning would crash down on some big boulders in the rear and send 'em a flying to little pieces, making the herd worse than ever to handle.

I'd rode in a few stampedes that was wild, but this one was wilder than any I'd ever been in before, the steers'd been rearin' to find an excuse to run for a couple of days past, and now that they had it was sure making use of the chance, and I couldn't help but think and wonder even as I was smoking up the leaders, how much a stampede like this, reproduced on the film as I saw it, would be worth to any moving picture corporation.

But I had to laugh at the thot of a camera getting that stampede as it was, even though I know how good they are with that machine. The lightning was playing on the steers' horns, and there was spells when it was light as day. It could of been photographed, *maybe*, but I couldn't picture a camera around taking it all, there

59

was too much real life and, somehow it didn't strike me as tho it'd belong on the screen cause the real good of it would be lost there, the life of it couldn't be reproduced.

The rest of the riders at the camp finally caught up with us as we had the herd slowed down some, and with the twenty cowboys circling 'em in it wasn't very long till we had 'em milling on one spot, we held 'em there for a while and when they're quieted down a little we starts 'em back careful and easy for the "bedground" they'd left so sudden.

The herd stayed spooky all the way into the railroad, and the double guard was kept up every night till we got 'em in the stock yards. We loaded 'em thru the night and at daybreak the carloads of beef pulled out headed for Chicago.

We was thru, and after resting up during the day and cleaning up towards sundown we was ready to take in the sights of what the cow town could offer.

The first thing that caught my eye as I steps out of the restaurant where I'd been feeding was the electric lights decorating and advertising The Palace, moving picture theatre, and I strolls over to it just to see what was on.

I hardly believed my eyes when I saw that the main attraction that night was no less or other picture than "Six-guns and Ropes." I near had a fit right there and it was all I could do to keep from doing a little stampeding of my own.

I wondered how much a movie outfit would give for such a stampede as I was seeing.

I reads all about the daring horsemanship of the leading man, and then I thinks a while, and thinking, it comes to my mind that it'd be a good idea to get the boys over to see it and not say anything about how I acted in that perticular picture.

I remembered the part I had in it as pony express rider along with the few close-ups, how I caught that wild horse at the water hole and finished my ride. As far as the doubling I done for the leading man was concerned I thought I'd best keep that to myself, but I was anxious to see how I looked when I pulled the horse over backwards, and when I jumped the other horse over the cliff or done the bull-dogging all in that leading man's clothes.

I cornered about ten of the boys, pulled a few out of bed and tells 'em that I'm going to treat the whole bunch to the show. That sounds kind of tame to a few, but I finally hazes 'em in and in plenty of time to all get good seats together.

I wasn't interested in the comedy that came ahead of the picture, but the other boys sure got a laugh out of it. As for me I was anxious to see what they'd all think when they see me doing my bit on the screen.

The comedy finally run out, then, daggone the luck, they went to showing all about how automobiles was made, and it lasted too long. Finally, and at last I see the fimiliar title flashed on the screen, and right there I changes to a better seeing position.

It started out pretty with the fiesta, I saw myself way in the back a couple of times and again when I rode and scratched out the gray horse, but I didn't say anything or give myself away by asking the boys if they'd seen me. I wanted to wait till they saw plenty more of me and hear 'em say, "by God, there's Bill."

The picture went on and come to where I rode the brown bucking horse in doubling for the leading man, and pulled him over backwards, and I hears remarks such as, "that boy can sure ride."

I was aching to see that scene where I roped Sam and pulled him off his horse, but that wasn't supposed to appear till near the end. Then come to where I jumped the horse over the cliff, and later on, the bull-dogging which all drawed something good.

I kept a waiting and waiting for my little part to come along, but the picture went on, and before I know it comes to the last fiesta and the end, — *I was left, and entirely cut out.*

I remember Sam telling me one time that they sure do plenty of that in the cutting rooms, and that sometimes they do it just so there wont be nothing going on in the picture that'll draw the people's attention away from the hero. Anyway it seemed to me like they should of left some of it. Why in the hell did they waste all that film on me if they wasn't going to use it, then I happened to think, and wonder; *Was there any film in that camera when they used it on me so free?*

Or was they doing that just to encourage me, and make me break my fool neck doing stunts doubling for that daggoned pink leading man.

I wasn't saying much when I walked out, but I still could hear the boys talk about the good stuff that leading man pulled off. Then one of 'em turns towards me and asks if I'd met him while I was in the pictures.

"He's sure a wampus-cat on a horse," he says, "and the way he pulled that pony over backwards and got up with him, you could sure tell that he's been there before and plenty of times. I'll bet that boy is a real cowhand off the hills, ain't I right Bill?"

"Yes" I answers "some."

I'm doing a heap of thinking, and then it comes to me that I'd like to see Sam again, I'd like to get him over to one side and resume that argument with him about the leading man and them what doubles for him.

Chapter III

DESERT RANGE RIDING

Ever since some of the prairie ranges wherever it was level enough to farm was took up by homesteaders, and the old cow trails was being stopped by the barb wire of the nesters, the cowboy's been on the move, hitting out for the tall and uncut and looking for where the hills was too steep to be plowed. The Bad Lands or alkali countries of Montana and Wyoming was and are still left as they was on that account and the range rider took hisself and his cattle to such places.

But there was a lot of cattle crowded into them countries and the feed which was getting short made it necessary to sell some, so a few of the stock men hit out with a saddle and pack horse looking for new range to the west. They scattered out through Idaho and from there south, where they hit the desert.

In them deserts there was already all the cattle the country could hold, but them drifting stockmen getting desperate didn't miss no possibilities for a new range and saw where with a little work developing the springs in digging them out to full force and putting miles of pipe line from each to the untouched feed too far from water for the cattle to use, that more stock could be run in.

With a lot of scheming around they bought out a few of the smaller outfits to get the springs and a footing. Others even brought well drillers from the nearest town and started digging for the necessary water. In some parts it could be got a few feet from the top, in other parts they had to go hundreds of feet, and then again there was stretches and long valleys with feed what'd make any cowman's mouth water for the want of it to run his stock on, but they could send the drills down to the limit and get no sign of moisture.

There's many of them big stretches yet where no water was found at no place and where stock can't run on that account only maybe a month in the year when the light snow hits it, but the stockman is taking big chances leaving his cattle stray out in it even then. That's in our Great American Desert you've heard so much about. Prospectors was sent out looking for seepages the same as they would gold. Them prospectors was mostly cowboys, grubstaked, and paid well if a water pocket was found where it'd run cattle for the dry months and hold 'em till the light snows came. Tanks was dug in the hardpan to hold some of what the cloudbursts let drop and with all the scraping, digging, and prospecting the crowded-out cowman found a few places in that dry country where he could run his stock. There was no beef raised, just "feeders," but he was a cowman and stayed with what he knowed. The stock didn't pick up no big fat, but they bred younger and faster and that kind of made up some.

Herds of cattle was shipped down from the north and east, along with them came some of the cowboys, all mixing in with the desert breed, and even though they'd run short of water once in a while and the ponies and cattle got mighty sore footed traveling from the springs or troughs to the feed, both the men and the stock enjoyed a freedom of unfenced territory and gradually got used to the burned lava rocks or hardpan flats the same as the native hand and stock what was there ahead of them.

I'd shipped down with a trainload of cattle and me being raised a prairie cowhand found it mighty hard at first, but it was all a heap interesting. There was no nesters or sheepmen to contend with here. There was spells when I'd give my whole outfit for a drink of water, but by the time I got to know how that fluid might be found by the lay of the land (even if I did have to go a long ways to get it) and traded off my angora chaps for "bat wings," I was getting eddicated some to what the desert called for.

I had to change my tactics a lot in riding and instead of climbing ridges to hunt stock like we used to do further east I'd got to see where by reading tracks the ground furnished all the information I needed. The country looked a heap different too, and I'd got fooled often by joshuas (yuccas) and other subjects, taking 'em to be stock, but I found that even the old desert hands themselves used to do that kind of unnecessary riding.

Like one time after I'd been in the desert a while I caught one of them old hands getting fooled that way and by a joshua. Them joshuas can take form of anything you may be looking for, specially if the sun is going down or it's getting a little dark. If you're hunting for cattle and horses, or if you was looking for giraffes and elephants even, you'd sometimes swear you could see them too amongst the joshuas. So it didn't surprise me none to see this old boy riding up the slope a good six miles out of his way and keeping his eye at one spot further up. When I come out of the yuccas, meets up with him and asks where he's headed, he points to where it looks like a white face calf standing alongside his mammy, then I grins a little and I says "I was just up there a ways, it's only a joshua." We ride down on the flat both laughing about it, but we don't spread it around none, for even though we knowed every rider makes the same mistake once in a while none ever tell of it.

Then there's the malpai, and granite boulders with buckbrush twisted all around, and on the desert flats the little stunted sage will loom up and look big as a critter. They'll all fool you if you don't stop your horse and watch it a while. In rounding up stock that way your eyes do most of the work, on both sides and ahead of you for as far as you can see. A range rider can tell a horse from a cow ten and twelve miles away. At that distance both horses and cattle look the same, just dark spots in the scenery, and the only way to tell which is which is by how they move when feeding.

When the sun is up at high noon and shining square down on top a critter's back and that critter is in high enough sage brush to hide the shadow it's pretty hard to see 'em very far. The same with a white, buckskin, or roan animal against the sun as it's going down.

I was looking for horses in a malpai country one cold day and was facing a strong wind headed for a butte what I figgered getting on top of to see the country around and any sign of them ponies. At the bottom of that butte there was a lot of what I'd took for brown boulders what'd fell off the malpai rim, and on riding closer I was some surprised to find that amongst them rocks near as high as they was and some higher, was the ponies I was looking for, backed up against the butte and sheltering themselves from the raw wind. The way the sun was shining on them and the rocks both and all a standing still that way made them mighty hard to see.

In the desert there's a lot of tracking done and you'll see the range rider of them countries with his eye to the ground half the time. And with one track near on top the other, cattle and horses might trail out in single file, but he can tell you within a few just how many made them tracks.

If it's a bunch he wants, he'll follow the trail a ways, see how long ago it was made and if it's a few days old, he'll get the general direction they was headed by them tracks and head them off on a high lope. The tracks might turn to the right up a draw but he'll keep right on a going straight ahead and pretty soon a few miles further the same tracks will show up again, and right under his horse's feet.

It may be late in the day when he gets sight of them, and when he gets them rounded up and headed back he's got thirty-five miles or more to make. The stock is drove back half ways or so or till they get too tired to travel, then dropped to bed down and feed. The rider hits for camp and reaches it along about midnight on a mighty tired horse, and it's close to twenty hours since he'd et breakfast. There's very few desert cowboys what takes grub and water with them and as a rule breakfast don't stand for much, a biscuit, a little bacon and a cup of coffee is about all the rider can stand at that meal. He'll ride all day and part of the night if necessary on just that, but it takes a lot of tobacco to keep him going.

Times like I just mentioned when a rider don't get in till midnight don't happen very often, then again there's a few times when if he's any kind of a hand he might have to ride the solid twenty-four hours or till he sees his horse won't stand any more, and he'll hit for camp only when his work is done, what *can* be done, or when his horse tires out.

The next day may be easier, a fresh horse is caught and the cattle what was left half ways out are brung in. They won't be far from where they was left the night before. And making good time, the rider can get in early in the afternoon, when he can kinda rest and make up for the long ride of the day before. That is, *if* some of the horses don't need shoeing or *if* in that herd he's just corraled there aint some calves to be branded.

Time and weather don't matter to the cowboy, there's the work to be done and he may have to put in from fourteen hours on up in the saddle each day for a week or a month till that work is done. Like in the fall of the year when the feed for miles round the springs is et down to the root, the desert cattle keep a sniffing the air for signs of coming rain or snow, and the sky may be clear with no sign at all (to us humans) that any moisture would drop for many a week but if you see the cattle sniffing the air and stringing out for the waterless country you can bet your bottom dollar that the ground will be wet in a few days, no matter what the sky says.

When they string out that way, they're going to where the lack of water wouldn't let 'em go before, where the feed is tall and untouched. They'll line out and travel for thirty or forty miles, taking two and three days to make it, and when they get there they're pretty dry but it aint long when the snow or rain will catch up with them, and when little pools form in the hardpan flats amongst the grama grass, the cattle will feed and rest up till the moisture is gone again, and then some.

Then when the water is down to mud is when the rider's got to get busy, for they'll stay in that tall-feed country as long as they can. They'll lick the little wet dirt that's left and beller for more, then a few lay down never to get up again. Lumps form in their gizzard and chokes 'em. It's anthrax and it kills many a desert critter, and if the rider don't track them down and bring them back that'll get quite a few before they start leaving for the clear springs again.

They'll stay on that new range till thirst makes them lose taste for grass, and when they start back it seems kinda hard for them to leave. They'll graze some more a ways as they travel till they get where the feed begins to get short again and by that time they're so dry that they make a grand rush for the nearest water they know of. They'll keep a walking faster and faster and when within a couple of miles of the springs you'll see them break into a trot, by the time they hit the troughs they're into a high lope. More than a thousand head of them fighting and bellering for a place at them troughs each spring has.

The first few drink it all down, some get hooked in the troughs on their back and can't get up, some drown, and when the water is all gone the others keep on a fighting for a chance to lick the bottom.

Them springs as a rule only have a stream about the size of a little finger and at that rate it takes a long time to fill them tanks. A thousand head of dry cattle can get away with a lot of water and being them springs will only take care of fifty head at a time there's quite a scramble for more.

There may be another spring a little further on a few miles, but the cattle seem like they'd rather stick round

They'd sniff the air and at the first smell of coming moisture they'd line out acrost the hardpan flats and be on new range by the time the rain come.

this first one and sniff the ground and lick the troughs for the few drops they get.

I'd been riding hard for days getting the cattle off the desert, cutting out little bunches and driving them to different springs where they'd get all the water they wanted without fighting for it, and one night here comes a whole herd stampeding for the troughs a few yards from my camp's door. I had a wrango horse tied up and even though I'm a long ways from rested, I see where I have to saddle him up and get to work again. I works and rides at top speed for a good hour before I can get the biggest part of the bunch away and headed for another spring. I takes the cattle over ridges, through junipers and piñons, and divides them up on two springs, and even though I hit back to camp on a long lope, the sun was up before I got there.

Way down on the flat there's more cattle sticking round the mud holes and the dry lake bed, and if I want to save them from that anthrax I see where there's got to be some tall riding, so with a cup of coffee and a biscuit to keep me going, I rolls a smoke, gets me a fresh horse and starts out for another twelve hours' work.

Counting the day before, that night and this day, that makes thirty-six hours riding outside the little three hours I used up eating supper, breakfast, and catching a little sleep in.

A few more days, and I'm just about through clearing the cattle off the flats, the mud holes are drying up fast and I know it won't be long till I won't have to worry about any cattle dying of anthrax for a spell. Each day is getting easier for me and my ponies, I'm just riding from one spring to the other branding up every calf what was missed in the round-up and some what was borned since. And about the time when the work was getting *too* easy why, here comes a couple of riders with their string of ponies and beds "squaw hitched" on.

We're to round up the cattle, cut out the weaners and drive them to Sulphur Springs, 60 miles away. One of the boys is a "rep," meaning a rider from another outfit what is sent to help round-up, cut out, and bring his outfit's cattle to their home range.

Three more days of hard riding and the weaners and strays are corraled and ready to start out the next morning. Then that night something scares 'em, they go through the strong corral like it wasn't there and flatten it down to the ground on one side. We aint real awake till we hear them stampeding down the wash and then it's too late, for by the time we'd got our horses down off the hill, saddled and after them, they'd be miles down on the flat and already scattering and mixing up with other cattle.

But a few hours later and still good and dark finds us riding down that same wash on the trail of them weaners and strays. It's faint daybreak when we see the first bunches of cattle, amongst them is a few of the weaners still too spooky to remember where they'd seen their mammies last, which was at the corral.

We get most of them that day and one of the boys is herding them on feed while two of us is working till way late trying to fix up the corral so it'll hold them that night. The next day we got the rest of what was missing, worked the herd over again and had them ready to start for the next morning.

The first night on the way there's no water for the stock and we had to stand night guard. The next night we was to camp at a well what'd been dug in solid granite a long time ago by prospectors working in that country. It was about twenty feet deep and where it'd catch and hold water from showers and winter snows. Very seldom it'd go dry being it was in solid rock that way.

But when we get there the second night we find by tracks where a big bunch of cattle had been round a few days ahead of us, some was still there, but in the well and drownded. They'd piled in on the planks covering the well, being they smelled the water underneath, and tried to reach it. The top caved in and it's a wonder there was only eight critters fell in.

We had our hands full with seeing that none of our stock would go back to the last water, and watching they didn't fall in that well on top the others already in there. One of the boys was kept busy keeping them together and where they belonged while me and the other feller "snaked" the drownded critters out with our two saddle horses. Some pull too, lifting a critter full of water straight up, over the edge and out that way, but our ponies worked fine and in a couple of hours we had the well clear.

There was a windlass and a big bucket to get the water out with and by the time we got our three hundred head watered, the ponies tended to, a meal cooked and over with, it was high time we hit our soogans.

What I've just told here averages up with the everyday doings of the desert range rider. It's *some* of what he has to deal with in handling cattle in that country, but that's not mentioning what kind of ponies he's riding or what kind of trouble *they* give him. They're not at all nice and gentle and waiting for him whenever he wants 'em, like I seen some fellers in the movies what only had to whistle and here comes the pony saddled and everything.

The desert pony don't come by whistle, for nobody has time to train them that way, besides there's too many of them. No sir, you got to rope your horse down there, unless he's hobbled, and even then you might have to rope him anyway. In your string you get gentle horses, spoiled ones, and raw broncs, they got to be all rode whenever you have a job what fits 'em and it's mighty hard to tell sometimes just what you're going to wind up to doing before you get back to camp. Like many a time I'd took a green colt or else a spoilt one figgering I'd have nothing to do but straight riding and find myself all tangled up with a big two-year-old "orejana" (unbranded critter). I could of let 'er go, but unbranded stock that size don't speak well for the rider what's riding that country, not if the boss happens to see it.

Picking a horse for a job reminds me of one time I'd went to work for another outfit in the Mojave desert country. The boss hired me in town and on the dirt street in front of the hotel drawed out a map of where I'd find the main camp thirty-five miles from town. "The 'cavvy' (saddle horses) is running about eight miles from that camp," he tells me and he makes two buttes to kind of identify the range they was in. Then he draws another map on the same dirt with the same stick and shows me where to hit for when I'd got to camp and corraled the ponies I needed to do the work with. According to the map I has nothing to go by from the main camp on, only two ranges of mountains what I am to cross and the Coyote Springs are at the foot of the third. There's no water between, so I got to make it in one day, fifty-five miles.

I rides out of the livery stable with a "company horse" and heads for the home camp, and I finds it easy. The next day I identifies the company iron on a bunch of ponies with saddle marks, runs them in and puts shoes on a few, fixes up a pack with grub enough for a month, and I'm ready to start out. I didn't know none of the horses but picked out a couple, one to pack and the other to ride, figgering they'd be gentle enough to trust in a strange country on. I didn't want to take no chances riding a spoilt horse just then.

I opens the corral the next morning early figgering to make the other camp before dark. The horse I'd picked on to ride behaved fine outside of trying to bluff me some, but I made him think I was too mean to fool with, so he didn't. We starts out and gets on a little ways when one of the ponies in my string, a big snorty buckskin, breaks away and heads back for the corral.

*I didn't know none of the ponies, so I spreads
my loop on the one that acted the spookiest.*

He keeps circling round it and I can't chase him back to the bunch. I know he's just doing it for orneriness and having a lot of fun with me, and then's when I begin to see red.

I builds me a loop, spreads it over his hammer head and drags him in the corral, telling him the while that if he's so rarin to be rode I'd sure accommodate him and then some. I see by the saddle marks on his hide that he'd been sat on some, but I could also see that he was no pet, cause I had to hobble his front feet and tie one hind up to get the saddle on. By that time I was seeing redder than ever and the buckskin bronc caught up with me in spirit. We was both wanting fight, and at it we goes.

I sneaks a glance out on the flat and sees the dust of other ponies a hightailing it for all they was worth, the horse with my pack of grub and bed tagging right with 'em. They was headed back for the horse range and just the opposite direction from where I wanted to go. The sun was getting high and God-amighty hot.

It's high time to be going, I loosens the buckskin's hind foot and he begins to use it, so I jerks him on his nose and flattens him to earth, takes off the hobbles and using them to haze him with, forks him while he's down, and up we come.

I'm working on him from the start and makes him think I'm going to eat him up, but he's just as mad as I am and he don't care much. He kicks my foot out of the stirrup and the spur rowel whirls like a buzz saw. It's still whirling and ringing when that same spur meets up with the point of his shoulder and starts making "hundred and elevens" (III) on his ornery hide.

About that time the corral begins to look too small for him. He wants room. He's bellering like a mad critter and his eyes shows white and red, he's still mad but I see he's getting scared and got more than he wanted. So the next time we sashays by the gate I pulls the gate rope and gives the bronc air.

Even that big country round us looked kind of small and we're sure tearing it up. We don't touch the arroyos none at all, just blue ridges and all of 'em seem level.

By the time we catches up with the runaway cavvy that bronc is willing to let me haze him where *I* want him to go. I notice the pack is slipping on the pack horse and it's tore on one side where he'd brushed up too close to some juniper or joshua, but maybe it'll stick.

We're all together again and going along pretty good, headed for that Coyote Springs still fifty-five miles away. The buckskin I'm riding acts like there's something itching him, but I have a hunch that's just because of him not being used to the saddle much lately, maybe on account of his orneriness. Anyway he was sure packing a big fat which showed he had it easier than the other ponies and I figgers to give him plenty to do to make up for his way of acting.

I'm looking for some kind of a pass where I can cross the first mountain ahead and not paying much attention as to how I'm riding when of a sudden I finds myself hanging on one side of that buckskin. He'd lit into it again and was bucking for all he was worth. I'd collected the "nubbin" and all the loose saddle strings I could get to straighten me up and I'm sure riding loose, the stirrups are a flapping and near beating me to death, my hat is gone and I see where I'm going to take a "squatter's right" right quick if some little angels don't come and put me where I belong.

And then, just when I figgered it was no use trying to hang on any longer and was looking for a soft spot to land on, a little jack rabbit scoots right out from under that bronc's snorting face. I feel myself going up, up, and up some more, and when I comes down I'm setting right square in my good old saddle again. The confidence returns with the new setting and I tries to pinch that bronc in two with a knee grip the likes I never knowed I had. My old spurs are up under the saddle skirts and I'm so mad that I reach down, pulls the bridle off that bronc's head so he'd have more freedom to do his worstest and me more licence to fight him.

It was no draw, that battle wasn't. The bronc quits first. His head comes up with nothing on it to

Even that big country round us looked kind of small and we're sure tearing it up.

stop him, and he's running away. I lets him run a while till I figgers he's went far enough and then I slips my loop over his head, draws it tight back of his ears, and pulling I takes a few turns round the horn. That shuts off his wind and he slows down to a walk, then stops, shaking like a leaf.

I slips the bridle back on him, then I gets off. I'm shaking too but it don't take me long to get back to myself, and when I straddles him again he's as good as pie and we heads back to the cavvy what was feeding and waiting for us this time.

We cross the first ridge of mountains, a wide valley and at the foot of the next ridge I runs acrost a corral. The buckskin behaved so well by then that I was finding myself rubbing him along the neck and telling him what a good horse he is, and when I comes up to that corral I'm beginning to feel sorry for him being he's getting tired, and I decides to change for a fresh horse.

I figgers by the lay of the country that I've still got a good twenty-five miles to go and thinks I'd better straighten up the pack some. I catches the pack horse, unties the pack and finds that one of the "kyacks" (pack bags) had sprung a leak, the bottom dropped out and left everything I had in it scattered out somewheres in the desert. It just happened to be the side where I'd put in all my canned tomatoes, and being they was the first I'd hit for and some precious in stopping thirst and hunger when coming in from a long hot ride, I sure felt like going back looking for 'em, but I didn't.

It was no draw, that battle wasn't.

It's dark when I gets to the camp what's called Coyote Springs but I know it's it from the description I'd got. I rides up to the troughs figgering to give my ponies a drink, and doggone if they aint dry as a bone.

There was about two miles of pipe line bringing the water from the spring to these troughs and somewhere along it there was a leak letting that water out. So there's nothing for me to do but trail that pipe line on up to the spring and I takes a bucket from the camp with me to make sure that I can get the water once I find it.

It was mighty good to find when I got up to the spring that there was another trough there, and working. But a bunch of cattle had got to it first, drank it dry and was licking the bottom for more. Being my ponies needed it worse than they did I chased 'em away and after waiting for near an hour for the trough to kind of fill up, finally the ponies had all the water they needed.

This second little instance goes again with what the average range rider has to put up with in the desert countries. There's one place where if you're a stranger knocking round and working here and there as you go, that you got to be a good rider as well as a good cow hand to qualify for a job and hold it.

Taking in all what you have to contend with every day, the ponies, the cattle, and the long dry rides to nowheres wondering if there'll be water when you get to the other end, etc., makes it kind of aggravating,

*The next water hole was forty miles, and me being a stranger there
I had to go on what I knowed of the desert to find that place.*

Roping, wrestling, and branding big husky calves out on the big flats ain't as easy as it would be in some good corral.

unless you're used to it. And you do get used to it no matter what happens. There comes a time when everything is took in on the day's work even if that day's work takes in all of the night with it.

I used to cuss the desert at times and leave it. I've left it often but always came back glad, mighty glad to see it again. Just *seeing* that country, going through it on a pullman or such leaves you guessing a lot, but when you live in it and ride all day long and part of the night as I've just told, in all kinds of weather on all kinds of horses and handling the splitting cattle all by your lonesome, you get to feel that you're a part of that desert, that you belong to it. And if you leave you'll come back like they most all do, for if you stay there long enough you'll find just what the painters and writers been trying to bring out and failed. That's what holds you.

And even though the desert range rider may be too busy to realize *what* a country he's riding in, and what he has to put up with in it, he learns if he leaves that he aint going out all together, for part of his heart is left behind in that wide, unfenced, sunburned country of the stunted sage.

Chapter IV

FIRST MONEY

According to the poster that Gill Bradson had jerked off a telephone pole, the Rodeo of the coming Fourth of July was going to beat any Rodeo that was ever held there previous.

It was announced on the poster that Jim Colter from across the state line had contracted to furnish the association with his string of thirty man-eating outlaws kept in shape and picked for their fighting and bucking qualities. It was claimed that three of them ponies had been tried by the best riders of the West and so far had never been rode past the judges. They was professional buckers.

Cowboys from that part of the country was to follow that ornery string of buckers to Romal and try 'em again during the events. A few trick ropers, trick riders, chariot teams and bucking bulls was also to be furnished by that same Jim Colter.

"Looks like to me," remarks one of the boys breaking in on the middle of the reading, "that we don't stand no show there with that crowd. They'll have two judges to our one and them boys know by heart just how any of them buckers are going to perform, they'll know how far they can scratch on this or that horse and still be safe of the saddle being under 'em, where with us not knowing any of them ponies, we're apt to keep a wondering what the horse is going to do next which'll hinder us some to reaching the finals, and I'd bet not one of us would even get third money on bronc riding."

Five thousand dollars was the advertised cash prizes, that was to be divided up in daily money on ten events and the final three prizes for each of them ten events of the last day. The first prize for bronc riding was five hundred dollars, and that we figgered was sure worth riding for.

There'd been two annual Rodeos already pulled off in Romal and this was the third. Me and Tom Sands who I thought was the best rider in the world was present on the first and second year; we entered for everything that carried big enough purse and after each spending thirty dollars on entrance fees all we got back out of it was mount money, five dollars for every horse or critter we forked. Of course that let us break a little more than even, but mount money aint what we was after, we wanted to ride off with first prize.

We was willing to ride anything in the world for that first prize, but somehow the ponies we drawed didn't buck hard enough and we had no chance to show the judges *how* we could ride. As it was we didn't even make the semi finals.

In bulldogging they handed me a wampus of a steer, short heavy neck and short horns and was taller by a hand than the horse I rode up on him with, me being a light weight I made a nice decoration for that steer till I finally got the right dig and my boot heels felt the earth again. According to the rules you had to stop your steer and throw him from a standstill, but so much meat all in one hunk wasn't easy for me to handle and when my little weight happened to get that packing house out of balance I couldn't help but take advantage of it. I hoolyhanned him on the jump and busted him right there.

A howl was heard, and a rider who so far had made the best time and was seeing the money slip away from him was doing a heap of objecting. The judges rode up and I was told that if I wanted to compete I'd have to let the steer on his feet again and throw him according to rules.

But me being out of wind as it was, I knowed I could never throw that steer if I had to stop him first, I also knowed that there wasn't any more than one man in that arena who could do it, not with *that* steer, but I kept that to myself and grins to the cheering crowd as I lets the steer go.

Yessir, with all our hard work me and Tom didn't get as much as a peek at prize money them two years. We felt that we was nowheres given a fair chance, and I for myself had a hunch that the outfit what contracted to put on the show wasn't taking chances of giving first money to any outsiders like Tom or myself, so concluded we was handed stock we wouldn't get anywheres with.

But this year's Rodeo might be different, and Tom and me figgered on trying 'er once more. We felt sure we could ride, rope, and bulldog along with any of the professional contestants what came with Jim Colter and his stock, and if the judges was halfways square, and we got the average of bucking horses we'd make the rest of the boys work to keep up with us.

The Rodeo was a month off, and that give us plenty of time to add on a little more practising even though we was getting plenty of it every day, all but bulldogging, and being that don't come in on range work we had to practise up on that when the boss wasn't round.

Tom and me was on day herd in the morning of every third day, and when we'd see the cow foreman line out on circle with the rest of the riders we'd get to work. Another rider that was with us would be our lookout and watch that the foreman didn't ride in on us, as the boss had often made it plain, unnecessary roping or handling of stock wasn't allowed on the range, and any rider caught at it would most always get paid off on the spot.

But we had to have *some* practise, and some of them ornery bunch-quitting critters more than called us on to do our damnedest, which kinda cleared our conscience even if we did roll 'em over. We'd straddle 'em as they'd get up and they'd give us a fair shaking, some of the orneriest we'd bulldog. After we'd let 'em go they was contented to graze on and stay in the middle of the herd. Tom and me figgered it done 'em a heap of good but we was careful not to hint to the boss that we thought so.

A couple of weeks of that and we notice some improvement, the critters go down easier, and one day when we borrowed a watch to kinda time ourselves we wasn't surprised to see that there was only one minute or so between us and record time. We figgered that we'd soon be up with it and maybeso break the record that was made by a Texas cowhand, none had ever got within reach of it so far, and we was sure that none of the crowd following Jim Colter could even hold a candle to it.

And far as bronc riding was concerned, both Tom and me was getting plenty of that, I was kept mighty busy on the rough string that I'd hired out to ride, and Tom was also kept interested in just taking the raw edge off the colts he was handling and scratch out the orneriness that was bound to crop out on some of 'em.

In my string, which as I said before was rough, there was one perticular gelding I was finding hard to set at times. He was a big black horse by the name of

"Angel Face," and looking at him you'd swear he belonged to some place where it was hot and the angels had horns. He'd throwed many a rider and he got me too, once, but I finally got on to the hang of his style and as it was now I could scratch him some at his best, and even look over my shoulder while I'd tickle his ear with my spur.

I saddles him up special one morning to see how wild a ride I could put up on that horse. Tom is acting as judge, and from the time I reaches down and tears off the blind I know that according to *that* judge's expression I'd won the championship of the world as a bronc rider.

"Bill, old boy," he says soon as he can get to speak, "if you or me could only draw a horse like that for the finals at the Rodeo, the purse would be sure to come our way even if the judges *was* against outsiders like you and me."

So we're feeling a heap of confidence when as the wagon camps within some twenty miles of Romal we finally talks the foreman to letting us go a couple of days ahead. We wanted to see who all had come to enter, what was the rules, and most who the judges was going to be or where from.

We get some information soon as we ride into the livery stable where we put our horses, and we was glad to learn that one of the judges was none other than Pete Worth. He savvied good riding when he seen it cause he'd been there hisself aplenty and we knowed we'd sure get a square deal from him. Another judge was with the Colter outfit and there to argue over the points with Pete, who was for the local riders of the country, such as me and Tom. The third judge, and the one what give the decision on whichever side he agreed with, was from nobody knowed where, and there we figgered was the snake in the grass.

We was willing to bet everything down to our boots that Jim Colter sure knowed which riders that third judge would be most inclined to decide in favor of, but hoping for the best, we was going to take a chance of getting a fair deal, and we signed in our names on bronc riding, bull riding, bulldogging and steer roping.

There was still two days to kill before the opening day, and Tom and me was making the rounds seeing who all had come in for the events, and if there was any present that we knowed and was afraid of in beating us to the purse. So far we didn't see any that worried us excepting maybe one, he was no better rider than either me or Tom but he was more of a favorite and a drawcard to the crowd, and as he was advertised a lot along with them buckers that was claimed couldn't be rode, it kind of give him a head start on us.

We was making use of our spare time sticking round on the Rodeo grounds and getting a peek at the bucking stock and busting ourselves getting at anything that was led in with a claim it could buck. We was figgering to be in trim when we're called on to ride and show our ability on the side-winding ponies, and Tom even borrowed a work horse off a team that was hooked on the water wagon used in sprinkling the track. That horse had the reputation of never being rode over one jump, so Tom took the harness off of him, put his saddle in the place of it and without anything on that pony's head climbed on. That horse lost his reputation right there and then, and we rode on looking for more of them what couldn't be rode.

· But we found some hard ones, and them was what we wanted — so, when the day come for all riders to compete we was ready to take on anything that was led out.

Everything started out fine that first day. Tom was up to ride that afternoon and from all accounts the horse he drawed was a mighty good bucker, but I had my doubts, as it was a big roan mare called "Ragtime," and mares as a rule can't be depended on to do the right thing, but on hearing all her good points I was glad to hope for the best.

She bellered like a steer when she found herself cornered in the saddling shute and tried to climb over the high wall. I had more hopes for her then than ever and I could see by the smile Tom was packing that he sure expected to have something to ride that was worth riding.

I saddles 'er up while Tom is putting on his chaps. A rider is next to me and helping by slipping the bucking strap round her. "Not so tight on that strap," I hollers at him as I notices him pulling on it. "We want that

She bellered like a steer when she found herself in the
saddling shute and tried to climb over the high wall.

mare to buck, not kick," and pushing him away I fixes it myself. I wasn't taking any chances on any of Colter's outfit spoiling things.

"Say, cowboy," one of the rail birds remarks to Tom, "better lean on that mare when you go out, she's a kicking bucker."

And when Tom climbs over to get in the saddle I whispers in his ear and I says, "You just do the opposite, Tom."

"I'm riding this horse," Tom hollers as he gives me the wink and looks back.

"Let 'er go," and open flies the gate. A roan streak of horseflesh comes out and in a running buck lands right amongst the judges and there she breaks in two, the earth shakes and the judges scatter like a bunch of quail.

That was one of the hardest jumps I'd ever seen a horse do, one that'd throw most any rider, but Tom was still there and when the dust cleared he was still a raking her and looking at any old place but at the horse under him. I could see though that first jump jarred the mare worse than it did Tom for after that she was just crowhopping.

I was sorry that them hard jumps like the first didn't last, for as it was I was afraid Tom wouldn't make the semi finals, not on *that* horse. Tom is working hard and riding reckless and the mare thinking she sees a chance to put in some crooked work makes another one of them hard jumps after which she acts like she's going to fall over backwards.

Tom is still fanning her and I noticed that his hand and hat went down to the saddle as if to push himself away in case the mare did fall back but that wasn't it, I know. The gun was fired and the judges rode away to watch another contestant that was ready to come out, and right then that daggone mare started to do some pretty work just when it didn't count. That's a mare for you, you can't tell nothing about 'em.

But Tom was sure taking it out on 'er, and right up to the minute the pick-up men came and caught 'er that cowboy was busy making that mare think she couldn't buck a saddle blanket off.

It aint but a short while after when I'm called on to do some bulldogging, and as luck would have it my steer happened to fall as I quit my horse and landed on him. I had to let him up again so I could throw him according the rules, but that first fall took enough seconds so as to put me back out of the money for the record of that day.

When Tom was up to get his steer I didn't want to think how luck was going to treat him, I was trying to interest myself by looking across the track into the grandstand. Something white and cool looking as the foam on a beer mug caught my eye, it was the fluffy dress of a girl setting up there and looking mighty comfortable and interested. Nothing of what went on was worrying her and if the way she clapped her hands meant anything she sure was enjoying all she seen. I was beginning to think that there was the best place to take in a Rodeo after all. Them folks up there wasn't taking no chances of getting skinned up or mashed flat, like some of the boys do trying to get first money and finally getting nothing but pains.

A streak of something went by and I figgered it to be Tom after his steer, but I wasn't interested there as much as I was in watching the girl in the white dress, she'd tell me by her actions all I wanted to know anyway, and somehow she seemed easier to look at.

A cloud of dust came between me and where I'd been staring, Tom and his steer had butted in. About that time the crowd and everybody is cheering and a whooping and I gets a glimpse of a steer going down.

My interest came to earth sudden, and in a second I'd jumped the railing between the arena and the track and I was right there alongside of Tom, I'd also got a peek at the stop watch one of the judges was holding and my spirits came right up with the sight of it.

Tom's shirt had been tore off him and as the steer was let up part of it still hung on a horn. "Good work, Tom," I says to the old boy as I escorts him out of sight and where there's possibilities of getting something that'd do as a shirt for the time being "I knowed that soon as I kept from watching you'd bring home the bacon."

At the Rodeo headquarters that night we learn that Tom had won the first daily prize for bulldogging — fifty dollars. The sound of that done us a heap more good than the money, but sometime later our spirits

Tom made her think she couldn't buck a saddle blanket off.

are dampened down considerable when it was announced that Tom was disqualified on Ragtime.

Tom was supposed to know why, and figgering there was no use arguing we stepped out, but we wasn't going to let it go at that — we knowed that Colter's pet judges had took advantage of that time when Tom touched the saddle as the mare was going backwards and called it "grabbing leather," and being that two carried the points against Tom, Pete was left a lone judge and his argument didn't go.

And what's more, we find out the next morning that Tom had been "switched" horses. We was talking to a cowboy who knowed all of Colter's bucking stock and as we're walking round the corral Tom points out the mare he'd rode the day before and says "there's that damn imitation of a bucking horse, Ragtime."

The cowboy that was with us looks the way Tom is pointing.

"That aint Ragtime," he says. "There's Ragtime over there. He's the best bucking horse this outfit's got and if you're lucky enough to draw him and *cowboy* him to the finish you're pretty near sure of first money."

That information caused Tom and me to look at each other with a lot of understanding. We was both grinning but not in the way that showed good feelings for the trick that had been pulled on us, for the horse that cowboy showed us was a big bald face bay. It was plain to see the Colter outfit wanted us out of the way quick as possible and they was afraid to let Tom have the horse for fear he'd put up the best ride, but right there Tom said we was sure going to make 'em run to keep us away from the money.

The second day was going to be a mighty busy one for me. My name was up for four events and I was glad to be in the "tryouts" in the morning which give me more time in the afternoon. I drawed a pot gutted runt by the name of Big Enuff and Tom helped me cuss the luck, but somehow that little son-of-a-gun could buck and he was making hisself mighty hard to keep track of. I was real surprised at the showing he made and more so when I learned that I'd made semi-finals on him.

Tom had bad luck in bulldogging that afternoon. His steer headed for the railing and went through it, leaving Tom a hanging on the remains of the fence. He was scratched up some, but his feelings is what was hurt the most.

My steer was better in a way, only he was too fast. He came out like a shot and kept agoing at the same speed, and when the gun was fired that marked the time neither me or the hazer could catch up with him for quite a stretch. When we did and I finally got him down it had taken too much time. The record of that day was way out of my reach.

In bull riding, our bulls just bucked in an average and the judges hardly noticed us, but Tom managed to spread a good loop in steer roping and that brought him first, where with me I only caught one horn and that don't count.

"It strikes me queer," I says to Tom that night, "why we can't do things here like we did on the range while we was practising for this Rodeo. Why I'd bet that we made better time out there in roping and bulldogging than has ever been made here. Yessir, I'm sure we have."

Tom agrees to that and is kind of wondering too. Finally we conclude that it's because there aint room enough, too many people to scare a critter to turning sudden and just when it shouldn't.

But we was still mighty hopeful for the next and third day we felt ready and able to bulldog the devil himself. We was going to make a harder try that day than any time before if that was possible, and *ride*. Old Steamboat would of been my favorite horse, for a real horse is what I wanted, a horse that'd carry me to the finals.

"Bill," Tom says, "you're going to ride in the semi-finals today, and you've just got to scratch your horse into the finals, that's all," and getting confidential he adds, "I know the horse you drawed and they say he's pretty good, so there you are, work on him, and if you make it interesting enough so that you'll be put in the finals I'll—" But there he stops and thinking I had an idea of what he wanted to say I tries to help him along.

"Listen, Tom," I says, "if the horse I get to-day can buck hard enough you know that I'll put up a ride on him."

"Sure, I know that," he says, "but you got to do even better than put up a good ride, you just got to not only

But Tom managed to spread a good loop in steer roping.

qualify for the finals, but in them finals you also *got* to show the judges that you're the only one entitled to first money, and to make that plain to 'em you know *how* you'll have to ride. There's a lot of competition against you and not only that but there's only one judge to our side, the other two are for their own imported riders, so when you fork your pony this afternoon don't forget *that* and show 'em that you are the wolf of the world."

Well I *didn't* forget it, had no chance to 'cause Tom was right there steady tagging along wherever I went, and he kept a thumbing me right up to the time I forked the pony that was to bring on the decision as to wether I make the finals or I don't.

Tom gives me another dig in the ribs just as I hollers for the judges to "watch me ride," the shute gate flies open and out we go, the pony abellering "I want you" and me awhooping to him "you got to go some."

That pony was a good bucker, he tore up the earth in good shape, throwed sand in the judges eyes and kept me wondering some. There was nothing monotonous about him and everybody seemed interested, and I caculated when the shot was fired and my horse was "picked up" that I was due for the finals.

I made a good catch in steer roping afterwards which brought me first money on that, and Tom kept his steer in the track this time on bulldogging, he made good time getting up to him and I could tell by the sour look on two of the judges and the grin on Pete's face that Tom had made the best time of that day.

It was natural that we was feeling pretty good when we walked in the rodeo headquarters that evening and hear the reports. We got out "daily money" and then we holds our breaths while we listen who all so far had qualified for the finals. There was only three and *I was one of 'em.*

Tom near went through hisself when he heard my name was on that list and a grin spread on his face that sure disguised it.

"Good boy, Bill," he hollers at the same time gives me a slap on the back that give me to understand he meant all what he said.

The eight or ten riders left what hadn't competed for the finals and due to ride the next day was drawing their horses and I edged in to draw my "final" horse, I closed my eyes and near prayed as I reaches in the hat, gets one envelope and steps out where Tom and me can read it together.

We pulls the paper out of the little envelope like it was going to be either real bad news or else information that we'd inherited a million, and hesitating we unfolds it. — "Slippery Elm" is all that little piece of paper said, but that was enough and meant a plenty. It meant that to-morrow I was to ride a horse by that name and that nine chances out of ten it was up to that horse wether I'd win first, second, or third money or nothing.

We'd seen that horse bucked out on the second day. He was a big black and reminded me some of Angel Face, back there on the range. His mane was roached and from what we'd seen of him he wasn't near as good a bucking horse as our old Angel Face, he wasn't as honest and we remembered that he throwed himself a purpose and near killed a good cowboy on that second day. What's more we learn that he can't be depended on to buck everytime he's rode, sometimes he just stampedes and it was told that one time he run through two railings and halfways up the grandstand where he broke through the steps and near broke his neck.

Putting all that together and thinking it over, me and Tom was looking mighty solemn. Of course, chances was that he might buck and buck good but the biggest part of them chances was that he'd just stampede and crowhop and then fall, and we knowed if it happened the imported judges would take advantage of that and instead of giving me another horse they'd just grin and put a line across my name.

Tom aint saying nothing, but I can see he's doing a heap of thinking instead, and watching him I can't help but grin a little and remark that everything may turn out alright. "Can't tell about that horse, Tom," I says, "he might buck like hell."

"Yes, he might and he might *not*," says Tom looking gloomy, "and I sure hate to see you take a chance on a scrub like that horse after you getting as far as the finals. If you'd a drawed a good one like that Ragtime horse for instance, I don't mean the one I rode and got disqualified on, I mean the one they cheated me out of, well, if you'd got a horse like that you'd have a chance for your money, but who do you suppose has drawed that horse?" he asks.

"I don't know," I says, wondering.

"That pet cowboy of Colter's got him — and do you think he could of drawed that horse on the square? Not by a damn sight! That cowboy is a good rider and being he is Colter's drawcard same as some of his horses he advertises and claims can't be rode, Colter is naturally going to see that that cowboy wins first. It's a safe bet so far cause when he drawed Ragtime he drawed the best bucking horse in the outfit."

"Now I'll tell you, Bill," says Tom all het up on the subject, "it's not the prize money nor the honors we're after so much, if they can outride us and do it on the square we'd be glad to shake hands with 'em and congratulate, but they're trying to put something over on us and on all the riders of this part of the country. Other outfits like Colter's done the same thing last two years and got away with the money when there was boys from here that could of outrode 'em two to one, and it looks like the same thing is going to be done this year, but if you had a good horse, Bill, we'd sure make them circus hands look up to a cowboy."

It's after supper when Tom, still looking mighty sour, tells me he's going to the stable to get his horse and go visiting out of town a ways. I can see his mind is still on the subject as he's saddling, and giving the latigo a jerk remarks that he can lose on a square deal and laugh about it, "but I'll be daggone," he says, "if it

115

don't hurt to get cheated out of what's yours, have it done right under your nose and not have no say acoming."

The next day was the last day, the big day, the grounds was sizzling hot and the dust that was stirred up stayed in the air looking for a cooler atmosphere. It was past noon and Tom hadn't showed up yet. I was beginning to wonder of the whereabouts of that cowboy and started looking for him. I was still at it when the parade drifted in and the Grand Entree was over, every kid that could borrow a horse was in it, some wore red silk shirts and they sure thought they was cowboys far as the clothes was concerned.

The riders what still had to ride for the finals went hard at it and I was busy watching and judging for myself how many of them would make them finals. I hears when it's over that only two had qualified and them two was of Colter's outfit, that made six of us who are still to ride for the grand prize, four of Colter's men and two of us outsiders and by that I figgers that Colter is sure making it a cinch of *keeping the money in the family.*

"All you bulldoggers on the track," hollers the Rodeo boss, and knowing that Tom is in on that event I takes another look for him, but I can't see hair nor hide of that son-of-a-gun nowheres, so I was getting real worried.

My name is called and I rides up to the shute. My steer is let out and for the time being I forgets everything but what I'd rode up there for. I done good time, the best time of that day so far, and I sure did wish that old Tom was there and seen it, cause I know it'd tickled him.

A half a dozen or so other bulldoggers are called on to take their chance and then Tom's name comes, but he's still among the missing and I see no way out but offer to substitute for him. I had a mighty hard time to get the judges to agree to that, but with Pete on my side and me atalking my head off, they finally decide to let me take his place.

I glances towards the shutes and notices a steer *just my size* already there and waiting to come out, and I also notices that they're trying to drive him back and put another steer in the place of him, a great big short-horned Durham. I rides up there right now and begins to object, remarking that I'd take on any steer as they come but at the same time I wasn't letting any skunk stack the cards on me by going to special trouble of picking me the hardest steer they can find. I object so strong that they finally let me have the first steer.

I was mad, and when that steer come out I figgered there was something to work my hard feelings out on, I made a reach for them long horns that I wouldn't of made if I'd been normal, the critter kept me up for a good airing, but when my boot heels finally connected with the sod the program wasn't long in ending. I stopped him good so there wouldn't be no danger of being disqualified and imagining that I was bulldogging a Rodeo boss or a judge instead of a steer, it wasn't long till I had him down.

"Old critter," I says to the steer as I lets him up, "you play square which is more than I can say for some folks."

I shakes the dust off myself, locates my hat, and being I was through on bulldogging I struts out round and toward the saddling shutes trying to get a peek at that long lean pardner of mine — a vision of his expression as he was leaving the night before came to me, and I'm beginning to wonder if he didn't try to even scores with the Colter outfit. "But daggone it," I thinks, "he should of let me tag along."

"You'll soon be riding now, Bill," says one of the local boys breaking in on my thoughts, "and if you don't bring home the bacon with first money you better keep on a riding and never let me see your homely phizog again."

"Bet your life," I says, "and that goes for two judges, too."

Comes the time when they're introducing Colter's pet cowboy to the crowd in the grandstand, and telling all about his riding abilities on the worst horses, etc., etc. A few bows in answer to the cheers and that same *hombre* rides to the shutes graceful and prepares to get ready.

The Ragtime horse (the one Tom drawed and didn't get) came out like a real bucker, he wiped up the earth pretty and Colter's top hand was a setting up there as easy as though he was using shock absorbers. None of the hard hitting jumps seemed to faze him and his long lean legs was a reefing that pony from the root of his tail to the tips of his ears and a keeping time with motions that wasn't at all easy to even see.

The critter kept me up for a good airing.

I felt kind of dubious as I watched the proceedings. If I only had a horse like that I thought, for as it was I didn't see no chance and things was made worse when I hear one of the riders next to me remark: "You know, Bill, we got to hand it to that feller, he may be with Colter's outfit and all that, *but he sure can ride.*"

A couple other boys came out on their ponies and they done fine, but it was plain to see who was up for first money. I didn't put much heart to the job when I gets near the shutes to straddle that roach maned scrub I'd drawed, but I figgers to do the best I can, there was no use quitting now and maybe after all that horse might buck pretty good, good enough to get me into second or third money but dammit, I didn't want second or third money. I wanted first or nothing, and it was my intentions to *ride* for that.

The judges, all excepting Pete, didn't seem interested when it was announced that I was next to come out and I reckoned they'd already figgered me out of it, as they knowed I'd drawed Slippery Elm.

"Judges," hollers a voice that sounds mighty familiar, "Watch this cowboy ride, he's after first money."

The shute gate was about to be opened, but I had to turn and see who'd just spoke — and there, a few feet back stood Tom, a glance of him kept me from wondering or asking where he'd been, his features was kinda set, and I finds myself listening mighty close as he looks at me and says — sort of low: "Careful of the first jump, Bill, and ride like you would if old Angel Face was under you."

I had no time to talk back, and that got me to setting pretty close, but I had to grin at the thought of the scrub I was setting on being anything like the good bucker old Angel Face could be, but I was going to play safe anyway and get ready to *ride*. If this horse bucked good, all the better — then, the shute gate flies open.

That horse came out like the combination of a ton of dynamite and a lighted match, I lost the grin I'd been packing, I kinda felt the cantle crack as that pony took me up to I didn't know where and I was flying instead of riding.

Instinct, or maybe past experience warned me that somehow and mighty soon we was going to come down again and natural like I prepares for it. A human can think fast sometimes, and you can tell that I did by the fact that all I've described so far of that pony's movements was done in about the length of time it took you to read a couple of these words. That roach mane horse was sure surprising.

When that horse hit the ground I felt as though Saint Peter and all the guards of the Pearly Gates who I'd been to see just a second before, had put their foot down on me and was trying to push me through the earth to the hot place. The saddle horn was tickling me under the chin and one of my feet touched the ground, my other one was alongside the horse's jaw.

I hear a snorting beller that sounds away off and I gets a glimpse of the roman-nosed, lantern-jawed head that was making it. . . . Old Angel Face was under me!

I hear a snorting beller that sounds away off and I gets a hazy glimpse of the roman-nosed lantern-jawed head that was making it — I'd recognized the whole of it in hell and instead of Slippery Elm, *old Angel Face was under me.*

Right there and then the tune changed, the spirits I'd lost came back along with memories of first money. A full grown warwhoop was heard, Angel Face answers with a beller and all the world was bright once more.

The judges had no chance to direct me when to scratch forward and back, I was doing that aplenty and they was busy turning their ponies and just keeping track of me. I'd look over my shoulder at 'em and laugh in their face at the same time place one of my feet between that pony's ears or reach back and put the III (hundred and eleven) spur mark on the back of the cantle of the saddle.

All through the performance old faithful Angel Face kept up a standard of that first jump I tried to describe. He was wicked but true and it was a miracle that his feet always touched the ground instead of his body. There was none of that high rearing show stuff with that old boy, only just plain honest to god bucking that only a horse of his kind could put out — one in a thousand of his kind.

I got to loving that horse right then. He was carrying me, kinda rough of course, but straight to my ambitions, and even though my feet was in the motion of scratching and covering a lot of territory on his hide my spurs didn't touch him nor leave a mark on him nowheres, he was my friend in need.

There's cheers from the grandstand, cheers from the cowboys and far as I can see in my wild ride everybody is up and ahollering, everybody but the Colter crowd. The shot is fired that marks the end of my ride and Tom is right there to pick Angel Face's head up out of the dust, that old pony hated to quit and tries to buck even after he's snubbed.

"He's *some* horse," says Tom real serious, "and Bill you're *some* rider."

Late that night finds me and Tom leading Slippery Elm and headed for the grounds, we was going to steal back Slippery Elm's double, Angel Face.

"Too bad," I remarks, "that his mane had to be roached to get him to look like this scrub we're leading. The boss'll have seventeen fits when he sees that."

But Tom didn't seem worried. "What I'd like to know," he says, "is how come I was handed the championship on bulldogging. I wasn't even there the last day."

"I was there," I says, "I substituted for you, and even went and broke my own record doing it, but" I goes on before Tom can speak, "if you hadn't brought in Angel Face I'd never got first money. If the Colter outfit hadn't switched horses on us we wouldn't of switched horses on them, so there you are, Tom. Turn about is fair play and that goes all round."

Chapter V

WHEN WAGES ARE LOW

I'd had bad luck that summer, and when winter set in and most of the boys was let go, I went along and instead of receiving a check like the rest of the riders, I was in debt to the outfit for one hundred and thirty dollars.

That streak of bad luck started when my old wore out saddle couldn't stand the strain no more and was yanked to pieces as I tied on too much steer. I'd got a few days off and rode to town to get me a new one. Wanting to test that new one some as I rides out I gets tangled up with a big muley bull, with the result that when the dust cleared it was plain to see for anybody else but me that the bull had got the best of the deal and me the worst.

I was told at the hospital that I was picked up by somebody who'd come along in a buckboard. I forget what all the damage was done to me but I had a mighty good inkling at the time, and specially so when the doctor said I'd have to make that place my camp for the next three months.

It was late in the fall when I got out. The company paid the bill but I had to work it out on wages which is how come that when the wagons pulled in I was still a hundred and thirty dollars in the hole to the outfit — that's a lot of money not to have when you're broke.

Having that bill to pay I starts out looking for a good paying winter job, such as contracting horses to break or the like. Running in my private saddle stock, I puts my bed on one, my saddle on the other and away I go headed up the Missouri river bottoms and towards the Long X's; they was running a lot of horses there and I thought maybe I could get what I was looking for without going any further.

It was a good three days' ride to that outfit. Towards sundown of the first day I begins to look for a place where I can put up for the night. I wasn't worried on account of me being broke for I knowed that all the old timers in that country then would of been insulted if any cowpuncher come along and as much as hinted that he wanted to pay for the feed and room him and his horse had partook of.

A half a mile or so ahead I sees a light that looks mighty comforting. As I rides closer I can make out it's a small log house, there's a warm looking log stable off a ways and from all appearances it looks to me like wimmen

As I rides out I gets tangled up with a big muley bull.

I puts my bed on one, my saddle on the other and away I go.

are absent from them grounds — and right then I decides on that place.

I admire and respect ladies a heap, but me being a stranger preferred to camp with the old single he wolf.

"Well, well, well — come right in, Stranger," is the words that greets me soon as I opens the door, "you're just in time to throw a bait with me" he goes on, and natural like, I finds myself pulling off my chaps and laying 'em in the corner with my hat.

"Larry is my name," he informs me. "Short for Laramie," and as a fair exchange I gives him mine. "Well Bill," he goes on — and from then on the conversation never has a chance to lag, it keeps up steady all through the meal, while we was washing dishes and on till bed time. He was sure making use of my company and all I could do was to lend a listening ear. The talk was still going strong when I pulled the blankets and tarp over me and I thinks to myself "great old timer," and that he sure was.

He'd rode up a horseback from New Mexico to Wyoming and started in the cow business there. That was forty years ago. Sometime later a hard winter near cleaned him out and he sold his holdings and what few cattle he had left and went to work for a cow outfit; then horses got cheap, too cheap to keep track of and brand, and about the time the west was boosted and grangers started to come in, Larry took it onto hisself to gather up a lot of unbranded horses, run 'em acrost the line into Montana and put his iron on 'em — he was figgering on meeting a demand that'd soon come from the new settlers that was already drifting in.

He met that demand all right, and so well that he soon could afford to pay a thousand dollars per head for a few imported percheron studs. A few years later he averaged three hundred dollars or more for every team he sold, and he sold a good many.

He'd only had one love affair, that was a long time ago and in Old Mexico, but as he told me, he still carried the scars.

So there was nothing worrying him much any more. He still had a lot of good horses, plenty of money put away and a lot of talk in his system.

He was some talkative through breakfast but nothing compared with the night before. The last of the dishes cleaned and put away Old Larry come out with the remark that he'd sure like to have me stay, for a while anyway, and let my horse rest up. "And besides," he goes on, "there's a black stud of mine out on the range I aint been able to find and I got to get him in before winter sets in. I thought maybe you'd stay and help me find him on account of my eyesight not being what it used to be no more."

Well, I figgered a day or two wouldn't make much difference anyway and if I could help the old feller out it'd be well worth the time I'd be losing.

He furnished me with a half broke gelding and we rode a couple of days without any sign of such a horse as he was looking for. He didn't seem worried about it, that

*He kept atalking of things what had
nothing to do with horse hunting.*

horse sure wasn't in that country anywheres or we'd
found him, and when I mentioned that somebody might
of run off with him (a thousand-dollar stallion was well
worth taking) all he said was, "no, I don't think so"
and he kept atalking of things what had nothing to do
with horse hunting.

The next day, thinking the old feller was getting tired
I suggests I ride out alone being I could cover more

territory that way, but he wouldn't have it, and finally he thinks we better quit looking for him remarking that some neighboring outfit might of run him in for him and was keeping the horse till he come and got him.

That leaving me in the clear, I saddles my own horse, ties my roll on the other and gets ready to go on. The old feller tells me whenever I come around that part of the country again to be sure and drop in and make myself to home wether he's there or not. "The latch string will always be a hanging out," he says, and holding out his hand for me to shake I finds there's a ten dollar bill in it. "Now Bill, don't get sore at me offering you that, your company was worth a heap more to me, and besides that little bit might help you at the other end."

Daggone it! what's a feller going to do in a case like that? But I didn't take it, I laughed and manouvered around till I made him think *I* was in debt to him and straddling my horse I made my getaway.

That night I'm forty miles from Old Larry's place and I had to stop at a regular ranch house where there was ladies, but I only saw 'em through the meal. After that I followed the ranch hands and riders to the bunk house.

Talking to one of the riders I happened to remark that I'd been helping Old Larry hunt for a black stud of his and asked him if he'd seen anything of the horse. "Why sure," he says. "Joe Henderson's got him on his ranch taking care of him, and Larry knows it too cause

Henderson told Larry to come and get him whenever he could."

Yessir, that old biscuit eater had used horse hunting as an excuse to keep me around and have somebody to talk to for a spell.

I was told that one time a rider coming through and stopping at Old Larry's place was kept there all winter when he only figgered to stay one night. Of course that winter being a mighty hard one and work being scarce far as riding was concerned kind of helped the old feller in keeping his company.

What's more, Larry was heard to remark one time that the hay he raised on his meadows was the best in the state of Montana and that a stack of the best of it was put up and kept special for the grub line rider's horses, but there he didn't mean the *regular* grub line rider.

For the *regular* grub line rider is nothing but a range bum. He's on horseback but he wouldn't qualify as a cowboy and won't work unless work stares him in the face and he can't ride around it, then it'll be just long enough so as he can buy a fresh horse and go on to where he can eat and not have to work.

The range folks never thought of charging anybody for stopping over night or even a week, a cowboy could come along and stay as long as he wanted to and be welcome, but the cowboy never took advantage of that cause if he was a cowboy he never was idle for very long.

There's two kinds of grub line riders, the real one is the hombre that makes a business of it. It's a good thing there's mighty few of them. The other is the rider going through and looking for work, even though he won't work for the smaller outfits he comes across. The top cowhand and bronc rider seldom fools with small outfits, he's scared to death he might be asked to irrigate or fix fence when the day's riding is over.

I was looking for work and the folks I stopped with knowed it and was glad to help me along. In return there was many things I could do for 'em that'd kind of repay for their trouble.

I might run acrost a cow bogged down, or another critter may've fell back into a washout, and me going through sure wouldn't leave 'em that way. I may see a bunch of horses and being it's natural for a cowboy to read and memorize the brands of all the stock he sees, it'll come in handy if somebody fifty miles or so away has lost 'em and happens to inquire of their whereabouts. A big gray wolf might come across my trail, and there's where a shot would do some good to the country in general.

So all in all the cowboy feels sort of justified in taking what his country offers and that country sure don't begrudge him making hisself at home wherever he's at.

I finally reaches the Long X's, and when supper is over I gets the boss to one side and asks him about ponies to break, but I'm disappointed when he tells me that on account of hay being scarce that winter, they're not keeping up any more stock to feed than they have to, and horse breaking would have to wait till spring when it wouldn't be necessary to feed 'em.

Seeing that job fade way so sudden sure took me down a peg or two, but I wasn't going to give in so easy. I thought of trapping some but the hides wasn't worth much, not enough to pay for the trouble, besides I had no capital to invest for a bunch of traps.

I'm doing a heap of wondering as I'm riding along facing a cold wind and headed to no place in particular. It looked like if things didn't change pretty soon I'd be finding myself riding the grub line for sure, and I thought before I'd do that I'd ride my head off, for any big or small outfit that'd give me a job. But I finds as I rides along that every outfit is settled for the winter and have all the help they need, there'd be at least four dead months ahead, and as I glance at the few stems of dry grass that's sticking up above the snow I know there's going to be mighty slim pickings that winter for both man and critter.

I kept on a riding and looking for work, I was getting to the point where most anything would of done, anything but herding sheep, and when stopping overnight at different places it was mighty tempting to accept the offer of laying over for a day or so and rest up.

Finally I did stop. I'd come up onto another bachelor such as Ole Larry. He had the same heart only he didn't have so much to say. It was agreed that I do a little riding for him and in the meantime snap out a couple of broncs he wanted broke.

"I can't give you no wages," he says, "but I'll let you take your pick of any unbroke horse I got."

I'm there about a week when we hears rumors of a dance and powwow that's to be pulled off at a ranch up river a ways. I wanted to go, only I was held back considerable by the fact that my clothes wasn't too good to look at, but anyway I was going to be ready in case I did go.

The next day I done a big washing. Most all my clothes was in the tub and on that account I had to stay in the house till they dried. My old "Oregon" breeches turned out good as new and lost their branding-season look soon as they hit the water, and after I greased up my boots with a piece of cow's bag and shined 'em up a little afterwards I figgered I could make myself visible to the female eye without hurting it.

Riders begin stringing by, headed for the doings, then there's teams pulling sleds that's loaded down with families and taking up the swing. Everybody seems happy, and getting on my horse I catches the spirit as I takes up the drags.

I'm invited to "visit the manger" soon as I rides up to the stables, and it aint long till all the world looks bright and everybody is my friend. There's quite a few others feeling the same way but before we all get to feeling *too good* the jug is smothered and hid back in the manger from where it came.

None of us that had indulged in the brown jug went in till the dance was well on and going strong, and then we was mighty careful for fear some of the

My old "Oregon" breeches . . . lost their branding-
season look soon as they hit the water.

fair damsels might detect the high life on us and give us the dagger look.

The evening is well on when, as I'm taking my dancing partner back to her seat somebody thumbs me, and I turn to recognize Tobe Bates, an old bronc fighting pardner of mine. There's a smile on his face that hides all of it as he puts out a paw for me to shake. I thanks the lady for the dance and taking the old boy by the arm I escorts him to where the crowd is not so thick so's we can have a heart to heart talk.

According to what Tobe had to say it seemed like he'd done mighty well since I'd seen him last, he hadn't got married but he'd bought a ranch and had a few hundred head of cattle, which showed that he'd either inherited a fortune, was good at cards or else had a natural talent for making four bit pieces grow into dollars.

When I told him what I was doing and how I was wasting good time he suggested that I come and stay with him, remarking that I may get what I'm looking for from the bigger outfits that's over his way.

A couple of days later finds me unsaddling at Tobe's home corrals, the old boy was out under the big sheds and busy tailing up a few wind-bellied leppies what had given up hope of ever seeing spring and green grass again, but Tobe couldn't see it that way. According to his language as he boosted 'em up they was going to live a few years yet, at least long enough to make prime beef.

I helps him get the rest of 'em on their feet and stuff 'em up with good hay after which we struts over to the house, it was a big house, not tall but rambling and covering enough territory to shelter a big family, on sizing it up I remarks to Tobe that he ought to have a long haired pardner to kind of help fill up the space and make things more home like, but he only grinned sort of foolish.

Winter wore on and Christmas come when Tobe and me went to another dance, and I got to meet the lady of his choice. I liked his taste mighty well and maybe it's a good thing he was there ahead of me, for I was finding it a hard time to keep away. Far as I could see there was no chance for anybody else but Tobe, anyway, and he was sure keeping a trail broke to wherever the lady lived.

Having covered the whole country for fifty miles round and not finding anything to do, I concludes I'd better drift on and hunt in other parts. It'd be three months yet before spring work started, and I figgered that if I could get in a couple of months' work or more before then it'd sure help considerable.

Tobe near had a fit when I told him I was going to leave, but I went on saddling and packing my ponies just the same.

I'm out a day or so when I runs up against one of the worst blizzards I ever seen. I couldn't see my hand in front of me and worse yet I had to face it, but I wasn't figgering on facing it for long. I knowed that if I stayed on the creek bottom where I was I'd soon run up against some kind of a place to hole up in, and I also knowed that if I got out of that creek bottom I'd be plum out of luck.

My feet and hands was getting numb with cold but I held and kept agoing. All of a sudden the wind stops, and straightening up I finds we'd run up against a log building with deep drifts around it. It turns out to be a stable that had been deserted for quite a spell, but the door was still up and working and the building itself struck me as good as a palace right then.

I brings my ponies in, pulls off the pack and saddle and proceeds to thaw out my hands and feet before they get plum useless. Picking up pieces of wood that was once parts of the mangers and stalls, I cleans off a place on the dirt floor and with a handful of hay for a starter makes a fire.

The blizzard still howls on full force outside, and even though I wish I had some hay to give my ponies and something hot to eat for myself I feel pretty lucky to be out of that storm. It kept on all afternoon till I rolled out my bed and crawled in for the night, and every time I happened to wake up through my sleep there was no sign that it had calmed down any.

At daybreak it was still going strong, but I could see it was dying down some and I had hopes that it'd be fit to travel in before a couple of hours went by. Not having anything to eat since the morning before I naturally was getting hungry, and by the looks of my ganted up ponies a little hay would go good with them too.

Leaving the stable after the blizzard.

So when the blizzard finally did let up, we broke our way out through the drifts that had piled high around the stable and took up the trail where we'd left it the day before.

The snow was two feet on the level and my ponies was having a hard time plowing through it, and daggone the luck I couldn't see a sign of a ranch building nowheres, there wasn't even the sight of a living critter, only in the snow right under my horse's nose was the fresh track of what I first thought to be a coyote's, but looking again I see it's too big for a coyote. A wolf had made that track and being it was only a short while since the wind died down, and the tracks wasn't drifted over any it was plain to see how long ago it was made.

That wolf wasn't very far away, and the snow being deep I figgers I can catch up with him easy enough. His trail leads towards a grove of cottonwoods, and I know he's headed there thinking he'd find stock which may have drifted in for shelter.

I rides in the cottonwood grove and can tell by his tracks that's he circled it to see what he could find, so to save time and gain on him if I can, I cuts straight acrost the grove. Sure enough, I'm still hid in the timber when looking out through the trees I made out his tracks leading to the opening, and not two hundred yards away trotting along is the wolf hisself.

I hit him the first shot. He went up in the air about ten feet and lit arunning. Leaving my pack horse behind I took right after him. I catches up with him easy enough

I hit him the first shot. He went up in the air about ten feet.

cause that first shot crippled him pretty bad, but it took four more shots before he keeled over to stay.

He was sure a big feller and pretty near white. When along about noon I finally comes to a ranch and shows the folks his hide, their eyes near pop out of their heads and I was afraid they wasn't going to get over it. I couldn't see anything extryordinary about that wolf, only maybe a little bigger and whiter than the rest of 'em, but to me he was only a wolf.

The ladies near knocked their hips down hitting for the kitchen when they learned that I *could eat something*. I was kind of glad that I had such a good meal ticket as that wolf skin, cause me having nothing but fresh air for near thirty-six hours was all set to surround a lot of vittles in a hurry.

I was busy dragging boiled beef and dumplings from the main platter to my plate which seemed always empty, and the while I was making grub vanish I was told of the history of the White Wolf, the one I'd killed that morning.

According to all that was said, it seemed like that wolf was the orneriest, wisest, and meanest of his kind. He'd been pestering that territory for miles around and killing stock for the fun of it. Naturally there was sure to be a band of coyotes following such a good provider, and clean up his victims.

The stockmen had all tried to get a shot at him, not only to get rid of the wolf alone, but he was also leading coyotes into that country and them coyotes was

According to all that was said, it seemed like that wolf was the orneriest, wisest, and meanest of his kind.

death on new born calves. But they always missed. A wolf hunter came down from Canada to get him one year. He brought ten big wolf hounds with him but when the wolf tore into 'em he left nothing but the remains.

Yep, he *was* an extryordinary wolf, and if it hadn't been for that blizzard making him more careless and his tracks plain to see, maybe I'd never got him. Anyway, I was glad I did.

I'm getting ready to leave the next morning when the owner of the outfit comes out and hands me a check. I reads it and I know what it's for, but I tells him the good care he'd give me and my ponies had well paid for the trouble I'd went getting the White Wolf, and I hands the check back to him.

"But," he argues, "that wolf's done me hundreds of dollars' worth of damage every year, he killed the best two-year-old colt I ever owned, and — "

"Yep," I cuts in, "that's too bad and I'm glad I killed him, but don't spoil things by offering to pay me for it."

There wasn't a stockman in the country who wouldn't have given me from twenty-five to a hundred dollars for just showing 'em the fresh skin of the White Wolf, but riding the grub line, even though I *was* looking for a job, and getting treated fine wherever I went, I didn't feel right to go flashing that hide and ask for contributions. Salting the skin good I rolls it up and puts it in the pack where it's well hid.

It's a week later when I finally bumps into a job, and the only trouble I had with it was that it didn't last long enough. There was four colts to be broke to ride at ten dollars a head, and me being anxious to be doing something went at it too hard. In two weeks' time I had them broncs so you could crawl all over 'em and they wouldn't budge. Of course they wasn't well broke cause it takes a year and some times more to break a horse and make a cow horse out of him, but that feller just wanted the rough edge took off 'em and gentled so they could be trusted, and that's what I done.

That was the first job I'd got that winter. I makes another circle that takes in part of the Yellowstone and finds nothing but a small job which paid ten dollars a month for shovelling hay to a couple hundred head of cattle, but I didn't feel like getting off my horse for that, so I rode on and kept a riding till natural like I finds myself heading my horse for the Big Dry.

A cold, windy March day finds me opening the big pole gate leading to the home ranch where I'd left the fall before, and somehow I was glad to be here even though I didn't come back rich.

The superintendent of the outfit hunted me up and told me that he's got a letter from Tobe Bates, and that Tobe said one of his neighbors told him I'd killed the White Wolf and wanted to know if I really did. The rest of the news was that Tobe was going to get married that last day of March and asking me to be present.

"Have you got the hide of the White Wolf with you?" asks the superintendent.

"Sure," I says, "want to see it?"

In two weeks' time I had them broncs so you could crawl all over 'em.

I digs in between my tarp and soogans at one end of my bed, produces the hide and hands it to him. He sizes it up as to length and color for a spell, and then he says, "Yes, that's him."

"What've you been doing this winter, Bill?" he goes on.

"Nothing," I says. "Couldn't find no riding that'd pay, only for two weeks, the rest of the time I been riding grub line looking for a job."

"Well, you didn't do so bad after all," he says. "This Company's got a standing reward of three hundred dollars for the White Wolf, and I'll give you twenty-five dollars for the hide if you want to sell it."

No, that *wasn't* so bad, I thinks. — "But the hide," I says, "I want to get it made into a rug and sent to Tobe Bates for a wedding present."

Chapter VI

"A Cowboy in the Making"

Come on, nice horse, I won't hurt you.

The first I seen of the Pilgrim was him a-standing on the porch of one of the cow-camps belonging to the Three Rivers Cattle Company. I'd rode up to that camp looking for work, and being that one of the wagons was to start from there that spring, I figgered the chances of getting on with that outfit would be pretty good.

The Pilgrim is a-standing there as I rides closer, and I can't help but notice the outfit he's wearing; him being a good-sized young feller it was all the more noticeable, and that hat he wore would of drawed my attention if nothing else would of. It was the kind of hat the Indians used to wear a lot, with real high crown and stiff wide brim; the face under it was round and smooth, hadn't seen much wind or sun. Around his neck and hanging down quite a ways was a big yellow neckerchief; his shirt-sleeves was rolled up; and at his waist was a big wide belt loaded down with nickel spots. The wooden handle of an old cap-and-ball six-shooter (the kind that shoots back and forth at the same time) was showing itself above that belt, and a long-bladed skinning knife was close to it. His pants was rammed inside a pair of "hand-me-down" boots with heels turned over, and a-hanging on them boots was a big fancy pair of cheap spurs, and they was upside down.

But that wasn't the best of it; that pose he was holding is what got me; it reminded me some of the movie comedy badman, and the way he was looking at me I was wondering if he was trying to look tough or natural.

There, I figgered, was sure a product of the dime novels, the best or worst I ever seen. I could see he sure thought he was some cowboy and that he hadn't as yet been woke up to the fact that no cowboy ever looks that way, and I thinks that if this is a example of what the outfit is hiring as riders, I'd better be drifting on.

I could see he didn't like me sizing him up the way I was, and, looking tough, he hooks his thumb up on his belt and close to the old shooting-iron. Whether that was a threat or a bluff, I wasn't worried, and still a-setting on my horse, I looks up under the big Indian hat and I smiles at him.

"Where can I find the cow foreman?" I asks real pleasant.

"If this is the kind of hombres the outfit is hiring," I says to myself as I sizes up the freak on the porch, "I think I'll just keep on a-drifting."

"I don't know," he says, but about then the cook of the outfit, hearing us talking, comes out and informs me that the foreman and the boys ought to be in most any time.

"Turn your horse loose and come in," he says.

The Pilgrim had disappeared when I got back to the house again, and looking around I spots him out amongst the saddle horses on the meadow. He's trying to walk up to one of 'em but that pony snorts out his suspicions and runs off at a safe distance.

"Did you ever see anything like that before?" asks the cook, grinning as he points toward the Pilgrim. "I know *I* never did," he goes on, "and when I first seen him standing in the door I thought I'd been drinking again, but when he started a-talking I knowed it was real enough. He said he walked all the way from Sandy and that's thirty miles. He was packing them spurs he's got on, and a chain quirt, and when he got here he drank near a half a bucket of water. I couldn't make out why he was so dry on account that there's plenty of water on the way, and when I asked him the reason, he said *he had no cup to drink out of.*

"You can think the way you please," goes on the cook, "but I'm sure there must be somebody camping on such folks' shoulder and protecting 'em."

It's sundown before I see any sign of the riders coming in. The Pilgrim is setting on the edge of the porch, and noticing me looking the direction of the dust the coming riders was making, he asks, "Is that the cowboys?" And from that a conversation started between me and him that was all questions and answers, I furnishing the answers.

His eyes was near popping out of his head as the foreman and the boys rode in; he was watching every move they made and enjoying a sight the likes of which I know he'd never seen before. He even forgot to look tough for a spell and the pose was plumb neglected till the riders begin stringing in from the corrals.

The circus appearance the Pilgrim was making couldn't help but be noticed by the boys, but that was all; it was just noticed, and even though there might of been a lot of wondering done as to how that *hombre* happened, or how hard it was to keep from laughing out loud at his actions and outfit, there was none of it that could be seen. By all appearances they just glanced his way and went on to set at the table that the cook had waiting for 'em, no remarks being made as regards to the new arrival.

The foreman came along, and giving us the usual once-over that's due to a stranger, followed it up with a "Howdy!" and the invitation to come in and eat.

The whole outfit had sized me up at first glance and had already took me in as *one of the boys*. They'd forgot about me as a stranger, but the Pilgrim was still to be accounted for. He was a puzzle and hard to make out. There was no sign of curiosity, but there was a still atmosphere circling that table that wasn't natural; everybody was quiet, and *there* was the hint or the chance left wide open for the Pilgrim to speak. The silent space was for him to use.

But the Pilgrim either didn't take the hint, or wanted the others to take the lead on the conversation, or else thought it best to keep quiet. Anyway, nothing was said till the meal was near over and the foreman started the talk on the work of that day. The Pilgrim was listening — and had no intentions of interrupting that I could see.

I figgered it must of took a lot of courage and rehearsing when sometime afterward, as the riders are gathered and talking at one end of the house, the Pilgrim busts in the middle of the conversation and looking straight at the foreman asks: "How's the chances of getting a job '*cowboying*' on this ranch?"

The foreman wasn't looking for that, and the question made him grin before he could think. Finally he gets serious again, and wanting to be easy on the boy he says: "Yes, I'll put you on if you can ride."

"Well, I can sure ride," says the Pilgrim. "I can ride anything." And hooking both thumbs on his wide belt he looks real ferocious, like he dared anybody to doubt it.

There's symptoms all around that his remark aint being took serious, and some of the boys had to pull their hat brims down considerable.

"Sure," says the foreman as he stares hard at nothing, "that's what I want, is good riders."

It was daybreak when we're woke up by the cook grinding coffee. We all take turns at the washbasin and the Pilgrim follows right in our tracks, missing nothing.

A couple of cigarettes are built, and breakfast is ready, after which there's no time lost in getting toward the corrals. The "cavvy-wrango" had brought the horses in, and they was all there to pick from for another day's riding.

"Are you looking for work?" asks the foreman as he hangs back from the rest and waits for me.

"That's what I come here for," I says, and after arguing some on the wages and finally agreeing, my string of ponies was pointed out to me.

The foreman is in the corral dragging his rope and looking for a certain horse to pile his loop on. A big, high-headed saveña horse is circling wild and keeping as far from any human as he can get; then the foreman's rope sails out and the loop settles over that same pony's head and draws up back of his ears; the other end of the rope goes around the snubbing-post, and as that horse runs close by, figgering on a grand getaway, the slack is picked up on the rope and he's stopped sudden. The snubbing-post had turned him, the same as it's turned and held many like him. He made a pretty picture of fighting horseflesh when he hit the end of that rope. His hair-trigger muscles handled that big frame of his as though it was a feather and seemed like he was just aching for a hand to touch him so as to give him an excuse to bust loose.

I've seen plain reading, reading of the kind that stands out in big letters and is easy to make at a glance, but none of it I ever seen was so easy to make out as what you'd get

161

with just a peek at that pony's head. From his quivering nostrils to the tip of his small ears made a "dead line" for all that walked on two legs and packed a rope, and them sunk eyes of his, they showed a hate the likes which I'm not wanting to feel against any human or critter. That horse was real poison, and I'm not exaggerating any when I say that a man-eating tiger would be a pet compared as to what the foreman had piled his loop onto.

"Where's that Pilgrim?" asks the foreman as he looks around, and at the same time makes sure the saveña has plenty of rope to play on.

"Here I am," says that *hombre* as he shows hisself and prances to the foreman, who sizes him up for a sign of fear. But there wasn't any. It was a case of where ignorance is bliss; and right then the foreman starts in on him. "Last night," he says, "you passed the remark that you could ride *anything*; well, here's a hunk of horseflesh you can try your hand at." And giving him the rope that held the saveña, he walks off a ways and turns pointing a finger at the Pilgrim.

"You took in a lot of territory when you passed that remark, young feller, and don't think I'm taking advantage of you with that horse, cause he's been handled already, and a few has rode him; but I *will* warn you watch out for all and every part of that pony."

My breath was took away some when I seen the Pilgrim take the rope and start walking toward the saveña. I knowed he was fourflushing when he said he could ride anything, or maybe he really thought he could; but, anyway, I was afraid of what that horse might do to him, and I'd been mighty glad if it'd been me that was to ride the saveña instead.

The foreman wouldn't listen to me when I told him how I felt about it, and all he said was: "Never mind, Bill; that *hombre* is old enough to have sense, and big enough to take care of himself if he don't go too far. What he's going to learn from that horse will do him a heap of good, no matter whether his ambitions might be to become a cowboy or president."

"But he don't know what he's up against with that horse."

"Sure he don't know, and he's so conceited that nobody could tell him, so I figgers in a case like that, strong medicine is needed."

Whether it was conceit or ignorance or both, that Pilgrim sure was short on knowledge and fear of horseflesh. The saveña was looking at him the same as a cougar would look at a wolf-pup — an enemy to destroy and put out of the way as soon as possible — only there was something about that enemy that kinda puzzled the horse, which was the whole of the reason why the Pilgrim wasn't turned to dust right there and then.

The horse knowed humans, but he'd never before seen any like that one. He wasn't packing the hated rope, and he left himself wide open to destruction. I think that horse was kind of hoping that human didn't come any closer, cause if he did, *he'd have to hurt him*, for even though this one was some different to the others, he hated him just as much as he did all humans.

The hate that saveña carried for man was natural. He must of been born with it, for as the foreman told me, all that horse ever wanted to do from the day he was run in to be broke, was fight, and see how much damage he could do to them that handled him.

"He ain't killed anybody — yet," says the foreman, "but that ain't his fault. The twister that first handled him was a good man and had a heap of patience, and I remember one time when the saveña flew at him with teeth and all four feet, that cowboy got through the corral poles just in time, and half his chaps was missing. That horse had the other half between his teeth.

"When the twister picked himself up and tallied up on the damage, he just looked at the horse and he says: 'I'll have to be more firm with you, young feller.'

"He *was* more firm, but there was no abuse done. A good cowboy never abuses a horse, anyway, but with all the handling we've done, that horse is only getting worse; but we'll break him, even if we have to get peeved at him."

Through all this talk we'd been watching the Pilgrim and the horse. A few other boys had gathered around, and we was ready each with a loop in case anything did start. The Pilgrim had been standing there, seemed like, wondering what to do. Something in the expression of that horse's eyes kinda warned him that all wouldn't be well if he stepped any closer. He'd

The lower bar of the corral was reached just in time.

stopped — both him and the horse watching one another, so the lead was left to the Pilgrim and there was the snag. He didn't know what to do. For once since we'd first seen him he showed sense. He was leary of touching that horse, and then he sees us a-standing there ——

Whether he was ashamed of himself for hesitating in what he'd said he could do, or the fear that we'd see through his bluff, I couldn't make out, but seeing us watching that way was to him a call for action, if he was a cowboy. I'd liked to seen him quit there, but nothing doing. The doggone fool holds up one hand, and talking away, he starts for the saveña.

A half a dozen loops was raised where it'd only need a flip to make a catch, for we was expecting that horse to come and meet the Pilgrim halfway as he most always did, but we was mighty surprised when instead of making a grab for the Pilgrim's hand when it was within a few inches of his nose, he just let out a snort that meant both hate and disgust, and circled away far as the rope on the snubbing-post would let him.

"God protects 'em," says one of the boys, and I figgered no better proof was needed as to the truth of that remark.

There *was* something in the actions of that horse which told plainer than words that he wasn't free to do as he wanted. "He wasn't acting natural," as the foreman said, and somehow we thought of a Protecting Hand on that Pilgrim's shoulder. His ignorance of the danger he was in called for a protection that wasn't human, and *that*, we figgered, is all that saved him so far.

He's circling around and trying to get within touching distance of the saveña, who's still doing his best to keep out of reach. That goes on for quite a spell, and most every minute we kinda expect that horse to turn and make a victim of that *hombre* pestering him. Finally he does turn, but not before the Pilgrim has the horse cornered and where he has to go through him to get away.

Four ropes settled around that pony's neck quicker than you could wink, but the saveña'd had no intentions of harming the Pilgrim. There was hate in his eyes when he whirled and struck, and he could of killed him right there, but *something* kept him from it, and as it was he just tore his shirt, knocked his gun out of his belt, and set him down out of breath.

That went some toward taking the conceit out of him, and when we helped him up, he'd forgot to look tough. Instead he was white around the gills, and I think he still had a vision of the saveña's mean-looking head as he'd turned on him and showed him the size of his front hoofs. Maybe he had a hint of what *might* of happened, but I doubt it, for soon as he was steady on his feet again, he remarked that he wanted to ride that horse.

The foreman got half peeved at that, not so much for the danger that was in it as for the uselessness in that greenhorn trying, for even though the saveña's bucking wasn't as bad as his fighting, it took a real hand to set him, and the foreman had no hankering of losing any more time and just seeing somebody get throwed. There was a long ride cut out for that day, and wanting to get things over soon as possible, he turns our way and says:

"All right, boys, saddle up that horse for him. If telling him that he can't handle or ride that horse wont do, we'll just have to show him."

The saveña was front-footed and blindfolded, for at the sight of us he meant murder once more; the saddle was eased on his slick back and cinched up to stay. All was ready.

The Pilgrim was shaky in the knees, but whether it was nerve he had, or just plain ignorance of what he was up against, one or the other kept him a-coming. We seen that he got his seat and told him where to keep his feet, along with all that was necessary to give him a fair chance, and then we take off the anchors that kept the saveña to earth.

The saveña stands there awhile, legs wide apart and every muscle quivering. His head is up, and looking back at the hunk of humanity that was astraddle of him — it was just setting there like a wart on a log not at all realizing what it really was setting on, and not prepared on account that it didn't know what to prepare for and how. If the saveña had only been an average mean horse, it wouldn't been so bad. My loop was built and craving to be dadded on that pony's head before it was too late, and just then the saveña bowed his neck and the performance was started.

With the chance that pony had there, he'd killed most any of us, but with the Pilgrim he just picked him up and tossed him out of the way.

I figgered it a miracle when as the first dust cleared the Pilgrim was still in the saddle, a miracle that the saveña had only made one jump, the longest, highest, and *easiest* jump I ever seen a horse make. What (I thought) could that horse do if he really set out to buck, but I could see he had no such intentions, and we couldn't believe our eyes when we see that pony just a-trotting around the corral and behaving like a good gentle horse.

"What do you know about that!" says the foreman, all puzzled. "If somebody was telling me about this instead of me seeing it, I'd just have to call that somebody a liar."

It *was* hard to believe, for everybody excepting the Pilgrim, but he didn't know the difference, and he thought the saveña had really bucked when he took him up in the air so easy that once. His conceit showed up sky high again, and the foreman, noticing it, figgered something ought to be done before that conceit caused him to take in too much territory and finally get the worst of a deal.

"Bill," he says, looking my way, "you take that horse and ride him around for the benefit of this here Pilgrim, and you," he says to that Pilgrim, "just watch that horse act up when this cowboy forks him. I just want to show you that either the horse, or Providence, or something, has allowed a heap, by the fact that you're still right side up.

"If you watch close, you'll see that horse act *natural* and according to his instinct, which wont be at all like he did when *you* was on him. This cowboy wont be making him buck, either. He wont have to. But there'll be something in the air which'll tell that saveña horse that he's free to do as he damn pleases this time."

The foreman was right, and soon as I climbed on, and the blindfold was jerked off, the saveña went at it and to his liking. He made a fast and furious circle of the corral, and run everybody out of it. I wasn't finding no time to fan him, as was my habit in such cases, and my spurs stayed neutral and away from that pony's hide. He tore up the earth in good shape, and I began to find fault with my saddle. I was feeling of it aplenty, but I'll be doggone if I could find any part of it that I could grip.

But somehow I was still riding straight up when a rope settled around the saveña's neck, and he finds himself face to face with the snubbing-post again; I knowed the possibilities of that pony's all four feet, so when I went to get off, I grabbed his ears, raised myself out of the saddle and slid along his neck to the ground. I felt the wind of his front feet as I did it, but I didn't linger long, and in another second I was out of his reach.

I don't know what-all the foreman had been telling the Pilgrim while I was riding the horse, but I think he'd been doing a lot of explaining for that Pilgrim's own good.

"The good luck you had this morning don't last," I hear him say, "and I'm only telling you this so as you don't get killed before you learn. Do you understand?"

The Pilgrim said he did.

From that day on, the Pilgrim kept on understanding. He changed considerable both in appearance and feeling. That tough look he was packing when he first come left him for good, and the reason was, that every time he did try to be tough or look that way, something happened which showed how helpless he was to the ways of horses and critters. He was showed how to wear his spurs, and when to use 'em, and one morning he come out without that wide belt which nobody wears but the greenhorn that tries to look Western. His cap-and-ball six-shooter was missing too, and with his sleeves rolled down and buttoned at the wrist as they should be, he looked natural and just what he was, not a cowboy — yet — but just a good feller, and that's all we cared, far as we was concerned.

Shedding off them ornaments the way he had, and packing a smile the way he did, made him welcome to the outfit, and even though he was of no use, and in the way a plenty of times, we got so we liked him a lot.

The foreman was inclined to show him the road out of the country at first, and remarked that he didn't want to take the responsibility of having a feller like him hanging around and getting crippled. "And what's more," he says, "I'm not wanting to start no kindergarten outfit." But he put it off a couple of days and then it was too late.

By that time the Pilgrim had got next to himself and figgered he should explain, so one night he tells us all about who and what he was — saying as how he'd always been strong on athletics, and the life of a cowboy had always sort of appealed to him.

"I've read all I could find about cowboys," he goes on, "but according to the impression I got from all that reading, it only put me in the wrong, and that explains some of my actions when I first come.

"I've rode a lot on my father's estate, and that gave me the idea that I was a master at it. I was, back there, but this is very different. Anyway, that was the cause of me passing the remark that 'I could ride anything.' I had no idea of what these horses could do."

"Sure," breaks in the foreman, "but you aint seen *all* they can do yet, son."

"I know I haven't," resumes the Pilgrim, "and that's the reason I'm asking if you'd let me stay on and learn. I'm beginning to think that cowpunching is quite a profession."

"It is that," agrees the foreman.

As the Pilgrim stayed on, he found that cowpunching was even more of a profession than he'd thought. Every day something happened where he'd see that it took nerve, skill, action, and years of experience to make the cowboy what he was, till he had a hunch that you had to be *born* one.

Like one day the Pilgrim was helping in holding the herd while some was being cut out. A big steer broke out and was turned back. He broke out the second time, only to be headed off and run back into the herd again, but when he come out the third time, he was wanting to fight, and he had a good pair of horns to do it with.

It happened that the Pilgrim was the only man that side of the herd when the steer broke out that third time, and when the foreman hollered, "Bring that steer back," the Pilgrim done the best he could.

There again he didn't know the possibilities of a mad steer, and all that saved him was the wise little cow-horse he was riding, but he wasn't going after that critter again.

One of the riders took out after him and dabbed his line on the mad steer as he turned to make ribbons out of him and his horse. Right about then the rope tightened up, and the steer was rolled a few times. When he was let up again, he was out of wind and there was sand in his eyes, but he could still hear, and the noise of the bellering herd sounded mighty good to him just then, so when he got back to it, he stayed there.

Riding back to camp that night the Pilgrim catches up with me and asks: "Say, Bill, will you tell me how long it takes a feller to learn how to throw a rope?"

Yep! The Pilgrim was all for learning, and he missed nothing. The foreman had let him have a few old saddle-horses and he was good to 'em. He'd noticed that we didn't run our horses unless it was part of the work, and necessary, and he done the same. In his string there was one wise old pony that could buck pretty fair sometimes, and the Pilgrim had been trying mighty hard to stick him. Finally one day he did stick him, and I never seen anybody look so tickled in my life. But the next day the ole horse throwed him again.

There was days when the foreman would ask the Pilgrim to stay around camp and help the cook, and there again he was agreeable and all interest. The big Dutch

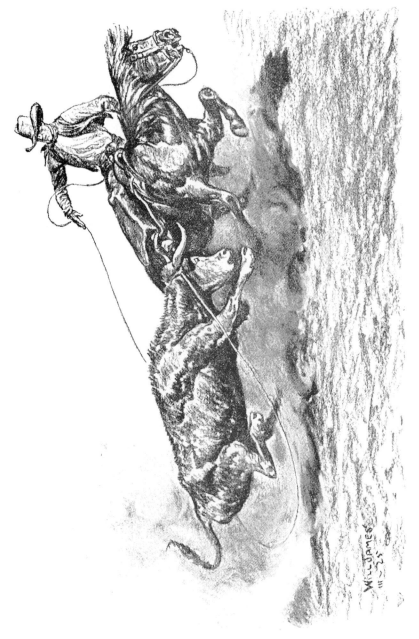

As the Pilgrim stayed on with the outfit and watched the cowboys at work he found that they had no time to spend in saloons, he'd read of them shooting up town lights and making strangers dance, but he'd never as yet seen it done.

ovens had him wondering how they could turn out such good-tasting grub, and he had no fear of sticking his hands in the dish-water when the meal was over.

At night, when the herd was bedded down and all was still, he'd most always get sort of confidential as regards to his feelings about what he was experiencing, and the general drift I got of his talk kind of woke me up to the things I'd seen all my life and never really appreciated. I'd been born and raised amongst all what he pointed out as wonders, but to me everything was only *natural* till the Pilgrim started talking about it.

"Some day, Bill," he says to me, "you want to leave this country, go to where there's a thousand people living in about the same space it takes to bed these cattle down, go to a big city, stay there for a while; then when you come back, you'll know what I mean.

Yessir, the Pilgrim was all right. He couldn't ride; he couldn't rope; he didn't savvy cattle; and he was in the way a lot of times; but he was all right.

He stayed with the outfit all that spring, and through the following summer till way late in the fall when all the work was done. He'd learned considerable for one so green as he was when he first come; his cheeks had lost some of their rounded pinkness, and he was lean and wiry as they make 'em.

The work was over, and one morning our checks was handed out, saddles was stuffed in gunny-sacks ready for the baggage-car and the cowboys begin to scatter. Some was for going farther north into Montana and Alberta,

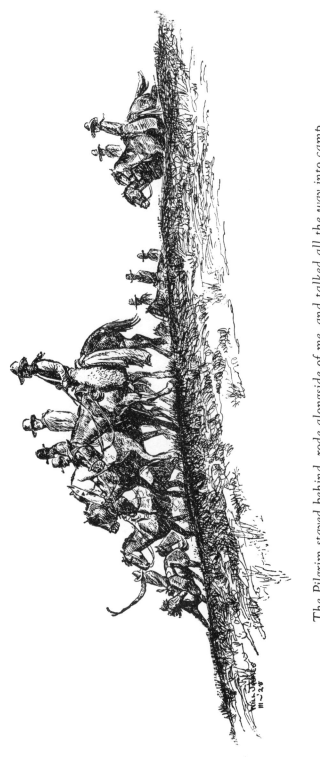

The Pilgrim stayed behind, rode alongside of me, and talked all the way into camp.

but most of 'em that was leaving the country for the winter was heading south, and me too. My next stopping-place was going to be Douglas, Arizona, where I figgered on getting steady winter riding.

As for the Pilgrim, his intentions was to stick with the outfit, remarking it was the best place for him, and that he'd learn a lot in seeing how the stock was being took care of through the winter.

I stayed in Arizona all through that winter and the next year; another year later I drifted into New Mexico and went to work there breaking horses for a big horse outfit. One spring found me in Colorado and the next spring in Nevada. I was just following the trail that answered the craving a cow-puncher has, to see what it looks like on the other side of the big blue ridge that's always out there ahead.

And it's early one spring four years later when I drifts in to the Three Rivers Cattle Company's camp, where I'd first seen the Pilgrim.

The place hadn't changed any. The same old chuck-wagon was at the back of the log camp and getting its spring cleaning before starting out for the spring round-up. Not a soul was in sight, and I turns my horse loose, figgering to wait till the boys rode in.

I walks in the house, and busy at the stove was the same old cook that was with the outfit when I left four years ago. After a "Howdy" and a handshake, he tells me of who-all is still with the outfit that I know. I learns the same foreman was still handling this part of the range, and outside of another rider the rest was all strangers.

The Pilgrim had left the outfit a couple of years before, on account, as he'd said, that he wanted to try his luck somewhere else for a change, but the cook had a hunch that he'd got tired of the life and went home — back East.

The foreman thought the same thing, as he remarked that night.

"You know, Bill," he says, "such folks as the Pilgrim don't last. Soon as the newness wears off, they quit and go back with the idea that they know all about this — that there's no more to learn — when at the same time they haven't started to know at all, and are just as helpless as ever. Some folks have an idea that you can qualify to be an all around good cow-hand in a couple of years, and where they get that idea, I don't know."

I stayed and worked for the Three Rivers outfit that year, and when once in a while the foreman and me would be riding along together we'd most generally find ourselves talking of the Pilgrim and wondering of his whereabouts.

"He was getting to be pretty good before he left," says the foreman one day, "and if he'd stayed he might of turned out to be a real cow-hand. I tried to keep him, too, on account I was interested in the boy, and I'd got to liking him, but somehow he'd got the craving to go, and I had to let him."

Come a time when our talks on the Pilgrim finally wore off, and it aint long afterward when we plumb forgot about him. New riders kept a-coming in the places of them that'd leave, and with the few changes that'd take place off and on there was nothing left but a far-away memory of the young feller we'd called the Pilgrim.

Winters come and went; spring round-ups and fall works followed; and steady, right along with the weather, I drawed my wages from the Three Rivers Cattle Company. I'd been with that outfit going on three years, and once again we was running in saddle stock and getting ready for another spring round-up. The chuck-wagon was getting another clean-up; new saddles was getting broke in, and new ropes stretched.

The days was getting long again, and evenings would find us by the corral till dark, where we'd either be fixing our saddles or chaps, or cutting up pieces of rawhide.

It was at such a time and place one evening, when glancing to the west, I spots a rider on the sky line. He was coming our way. I looks up again when I thinks he is close enough to identify. There was something sort of familiar about him, but right then I couldn't do any placing, and it's not till he rides closer that I makes him out — the Pilgrim.

And he didn't look at all like a pilgrim no more. He was just quiet and Western, but there was no mistaking that grin of his as he seen me.

The foreman was next after me as I went out to meet him, and when he reached the spot that me and the

Pilgrim was holding down, there was no chance for grass to grow there for quite a spell.

The conversation covered three or four years of time, and it run steady till the beds was unrolled and everybody crawled in. We was glad to hear that the Pilgrim had stayed West and worked on with different outfits till, as he put it, he could qualify as an average with the range riders.

The foreman is grinning some, and pretty soon he asks:

"Do you still think you can ride *anything?*"

"No," says the Pilgrim, laughing. "It's been proved about fifty times that I couldn't, but there's one horse I'd like to try again just to see if I do qualify, and that's the saveña. Is he still with the outfit?"

"You bet he is, son — and I'll let you play with him in the morning, all you want," says the foreman.

On account of his orneriness, the saveña had been having it mighty easy. He was, according, fat as a seal but as mean as ever. He'd been rode a few times since that morning of the Pilgrim's tryout, but he fought so much in saddling and done so much bucking afterward, that every time he had to be turned loose again, he'd be all in and not fit to ride out on a day's work.

He hadn't hurt nobody lately, but that wasn't his fault, for nobody give him the chance. So, as it was, the Pilgrim had the same horse to test his ability on as he'd had some six years or more before, only the horse might act different this time. It all depended on that horse's ability, or what the Pilgrim had learned.

There was no mistaking but what the Pilgrim *had* learnt considerable through them years of steady work. The proof of that was in every step he made. There was confidence plain to see, and when he opened the corral gate the next morning and unlimbered his rope to snare the saveña, I didn't have none of the worried feeling that I'd had that morning, six years past.

Nothing was holding the saveña back this time; he acted natural. A rope was holding him to the snubbing-post, and when he showed his teeth and went to reaching for the Pilgrim with his front feet, another rope took them front feet away from him and he was layed flat to earth.

He bellered his hate for the Pilgrim while that *hombre*, cool as a December morning, was drawing the cinch of his saddle under the saveña. All by his lonesome he saddled him and eased a hackamore on the mean-looking head. Not a false move he made, and when he straddled all he could of the saveña, which is kinda hard to do in that laying position, and all was set for us to take off the rope that'd leave the horse free to go, that boy was packing a smile we was glad to see, for it was a cowboy's smile, when the cowboy is at the height of his glory and rarin' to go.

The saveña was free, and he went up as though there'd been steel springs boosting him from the start. He bucked good and stayed in one spot, and he sure made good use of all the atmosphere and space that was in that one spot. Every once in a while we'd hear a spur-rowel sing; the saveña had reached up while in midair and kicked it.

Yessir! That horse meant business, and we didn't want to think of what would happen right then if the Pilgrim lost his seat. We could see it was the saveña's ambitions to have the boy under his feet for just one second.

But that boy wasn't worried, far as we could see. If anything, he was sure enjoying hisself. He kept a-reefing the saveña and a-smiling, and only once did I see him reach down as though he wanted to choke the saddle-horn, but he didn't; he rode over the ruffle easy enough and with his hat he sure dusted that pony as though he was in need of it.

But the ticklish spell was still to come. The saveña had quit bucking, and like a wolf at a gopher-hole he was waiting for the Pilgrim to leave the saddle; that was to be his last chance to do some exterminating.

Of a sudden the saveña feels both his ears grabbed and twisted in a way which for the time being separates him from his thoughts of damage —

In another second the Pilgrim is on the ground and making far-apart tracks toward the corral bars. It aint till then that the saveña comes to, and seeing his victim getting away he makes a running jump that puts him within reach. But he was just a shade too late, and when we helped the Pilgrim through the corral and on the other side, only part of his shirt was missing.

The Pilgrim was a pilgrim no longer.

Chapter VII

HIS WATERLOO

"**Y**ou know Dave Simmons, don't you?" asks the cow foreman as he drags a chair towards where I'm setting away to one corner of the bunk house and rolling a smoke to kinda put the finishing touches on the good supper I'd just had.

"Never heard of him," I says as I lights my cigarette and leans back. "I'm a stranger around here."

"You sure must be a stranger and from far away not to 've heard of Dave," he says, looking at me sort of surprised.

"Why," he goes on, "Dave is as well known in this state as our governor, and not only in this state either, folks know him plum up to the Canadian line; of course his reputation has died down some these last couple of years on account of new folks dropping in steady and grabbing all the honors, and you being a young feller and after Dave's time kinda excuses you for not knowing of him.

"But what I'm getting at is this, about two days ride north from here is the prettiest camp this outfit's got. Well, Dave's up at that camp and keeping tab on some thoroughbred Hereford cattle. He's had that job now for some time; and there's where you'll be going with the broncs I hired you to break. We've rounded up near a hundred head of colts around here from three years old on up, that's to be rode, and I think that'll keep you busy for many months. You'll be staying up there with Dave, that's why I asked you if you knowed him. He'll be glad to help you whenever you give him the chance, and being there's good corrals there and a fine country around to ride broncs in, you two sure ought to be able to enjoy yourselves.

"Now, being that you and Dave will have to batch it together you ought to know some about him. But I sure can't get over the fact that you never heard of that old boy, and it makes me ask, where are you from, young feller?"

"Montana is my home state," I says, "but I'm from most anywheres along the Rockies."

"Sure queer you and Dave never crossed trails — and when I first set my eyes on you riding that ornery gelding back of McAllister's stable at Miles I thought of Dave and how he'd like to seen you ride that horse; your riding reminded me of him, so slick and free and easy it was.

That's what made me ask if you wanted a job snapping
broncs. Dave always did admire good riding.

"I remember one time when Dave was a younger feller,
he'd met a duke or something up in Canada what claimed
there was a stallion back in England that no human could
ride; there was a few thousand dollars put up by the
owners of that horse that said the same thing, and that
got Dave all riled up. He was rarin' to go and see that
pony and it wasn't but a few weeks when he did cross the
water, his little saddle right with him, too.

"Well, a good two months went by and nary a word
did we hear from that hombre. We'd got to thinking that
stallion had got the best of him and just about decided to
investigate when we get a letter from him and a clipping
of newspaper telling about the wonderful horsemanship
of Dave Simmons that American cowboy. It went on and
told of the fight between brute strength and human skill
and cunning, the desperate chances Dave was taking to
curb down the viciousness of that outlaw horse and how
for a spell it looked like the stallion was going to come
out victorious. But finally and after a hard fight the iron
muscles of that horse had to give in under the steel brawn
of the cowboy that was a-settin' on top of him, the earth-
shakin' bucks slowed down gradual to crowhops, and
head down, nostrils a-quivering, sweat a-dripping from
all over him, the horse stopped, the cowboy dismounted
with a smile and crowds cheered the victor.

"'The worst horse ever known had been conquered,'
says the paper, but here's what Dave said in his letter:

'That pony could buck pretty good alright, but he was nothing much compared to Old Sox.' Old Sox was a horse Dave had started to break before he left, but Dave had seen many a harder horse to ride than even Sox ever was.

"Anyway Dave went on in his letter and said how he wished he had Sox along so as he could show them folks what real fighting horseflesh acted like, 'but they was satisfied,' he says, 'and they was all good to me. Even when I was handed the three thousand dollars reward they congratulated and remarked that the show was well worth the money.'

"Dave was hoping there was more easy money like that hanging around and even thought of shipping some of our own ponies over there so he'd get a chance to ride 'em, but it took him a lot of money to get back and when he reached Chicago a few months later he was broke flat. He rode a few mean horses that'd been shipped there from the range and by manouvering around he got enough money out of it to get back to the outfit.

"'Well,' he says as I met him at the train, 'I sure had a lot of fun anyway and seen plenty of sights. I think I'll go to work now and be good, but it sure gets under my skin when I think of the ponies I got to ride here for fifty dollars a month. I figger at the rate I'm riding here which is ten broncs a day I only get seventeen cents per mount, that's not much compared to three thousand dollars, and any of these broncs are as bad as that English stallion, and many are a heap worse, besides there's no folks sticking around these bare corrals to cheer when I put up a good ride.'

"But Dave was too much of a cowboy to let any brass band spoil him, and with all the lamenting he done there was a grin following. I could see he was glad to get back and it was no time when England and the 'chaps' over there was only distant memory.

"Dave was born and raised in the Buffalo Basin country. His dad had a nice bunch of cattle and from the time Dave was fourteen years old he was kept busy riding. He started breaking horses at home and it wasn't long when he was breaking 'em for neighbors and using 'em on his dad's range. From the time he was fifteen Dave was never seen riding a gentle horse and soon as the pony under him quit his fighting and bucking he'd turn that horse over as broke and run in another green bronc.

"He started in like all cowboys do, only he got to be a way better rider than the average. There was many a horse throwed him at first, and many a shirt his mother had to mend, but never did I see the horse Dave was afraid of.

"He was along about eighteen when he came to work for this outfit, and a more reckless rider I've never seen. Many is the time I've watched him get on a raw bronc in a winter day. He'd get the barefooted horse on a slick patch of ice and climb on him when it was all the horse could do to stand up.

"'That's a fine place to see how good this bronc is on his feet,' he'd remark, and as luck would have it the horse would seldom fall. If I'd tried a stunt like that I know I'd never come out of it without a broken leg.

"I've often seen him take his rope down on a colt when it'd be the first time that colt was rode, and rope some full-grown critter — it didn't matter to him what kind of country he was in at the time either, and whether it was open flat or rocky steep ridges covered with timber, it was all the same to Dave.

"His rope was always tied hard and fast to his saddle horn when he snared anything, and that I think is the most dangerous thing a man can do on an unbroke horse; he'd get in mix-ups that way that couldn't be watched for the dust that was stirred, but the first thing you'd see when that dust settled was Dave's head a-smiling and watching the conglomeration of a horse and critter all mixed with a rope.

"Why one time I seen him rope a little calf that'd broke away from the herd, and as usual he was riding a mighty mean horse. That little calf was sure running for a ways and when Dave caught him it was quite a distance back to the herd. The little calf was only a week or so old and of course he didn't want to drag him back all the way — well sir, that daggone fool just pulls on the rope and hoists the calf right up in the saddle with him.

"His horse started to bucking, and believe me, stranger, that horse could sure buck, too. But Dave didn't want him to, right then, and that pony having had previous experience with that hombre straightened up and lit out a-crowhopping and running. I bet that was the wildest ride any calf ever had, but he was took back to his mammy alright even though the horse that packed him did have murder in his eye.

"Of course we all know that a cowboy, to be one, has to be mighty reckless and carefree as regards to life and limb; I've had many a good cowboy on this outfit; that's all I'd ever keep. But I don't expect none of 'em to carry on the standard that Dave has set. I've knowed many riders that tallied up pretty well with him, but somehow Dave was always a leetle bit better.

"I've stood and watched Dave handle green broncs by the hour. The way he'd go at it always done my heart a lot of good. He was so quiet that you wouldn't know he was around unless you seen him; he never petted a horse, but he done better: he treated 'em like they knowed something. And it'd always wind up by them ponies just a-busting themselves to do things they knowed Dave wanted 'em to do.

"Yes sir! he was a great hand. He never made a horse buck but he never was so happy as when some pony would buck with him. The harder the tossing the more he'd grin, and I never seen a feller so disappointed as when he'd get on a fat, kinky, raw bronc and that horse didn't bog his head and buck good on first setting. He'd always pass this remark as he'd pull off his riggin': 'That horse'll never be worth a damn.'

"But few ever disappointed him that way. He believed that all horses had some buck in 'em and the time to get it out of their system was on first saddlings; and he'd often say: 'Look out for the horse that don't jump when he's first rode, he'll break in two just when you think you're riding something gentle. And when them kind of ponies do break in two in that stage of the game they're most generally hard to set, and a lot harder to make 'em quit it.'

"As for the horse that never no time bucked, he'd wave his hand and say: 'Take 'em away, feed 'em sugar and sell 'em off to some livery stable.'"

Right about then I broke in on the foreman and asked: "Did Dave ever run acrost any horse that was too much for him?"

"No, sir," says he, "not since he was fifteen and while he was *riding*. Of course, like the rest of us he finally had to quit, but I'll come to that later, and as I was going to say ——

"One spring we'd bought a carload of Oregon horses. We'd got 'em cheap and figgered they'd make fine saddle stock. They was all well built ponies and averaging around eleven hundred with just enough daylight under 'em to make 'em good anywheres they was put. Their age run from three to ten and even twelve years old, and none of 'em was supposed to've been rode.

"But soon as we got 'em in our own corrals we found that about half of 'em had been tampered with and turned

194

out to be real outlaws; that's why we got 'em cheap. Of course we never worried much about that cause we knowed we had a man that'd be glad to get a chance at 'em. He enjoyed that kind, and we felt mighty sure that he'd make good ponies out of the worst of 'em.

"And that's what Dave did. He lit into them broncs and whistled a tune while they fought and bucked and tore the buttons off his shirt with their front feet. Dave had a way of always being where them broncs didn't want him to be, and when they'd strike or kick there was always a hair's breadth between the hoof and what that hoof tried to reach.

"Dave let 'em buck and fight all they wanted, and when they'd quit he'd make them broncs feel like they hadn't done anything. It sure got under their hide to see that their efforts to orneriness didn't faze that human none at all; instead he seemed to like it and called for more.

"Like one morning Dave walked into the corral, roped the meanest one of the bunch and saddled him while that pony was near tearing hisself apart a-trying to outdo that human and take the grin out of his face with new tricks. He was a big powerful 'gruller' horse, tall and rawboned and all muscle. But with all his strength, action, meanness, and size, Dave was never interrupted no time, and while the big gray was a-standing stary-eyed for a second and wondering what to do next Dave climbed him and unloosened the foot rope.

"It all was done so neat and quick and easy that the horse didn't even know where his man went till he looked back and seen him a-setting there right on his middle and a-grinning — well, sir, that horse was desperate. You could see it in every inch of his long frame; he didn't know whether to just stand still and quiver or just leave the earth for good.

"A beller came out of him that made every animal within hearing distance stop grazing and stand still with head up and a-wondering. Such a beller had been heard before, but only in mountain lion countries and when the big cat had jumped down on his victim. If it'd been a mountain lion that big horse could of shed him off, maybe, but it was sure aggravating how that human could stick and laugh at him through the hard crooked jumps that'd jarred loose every other rider.

"I know that horse bucked then like he never did before; he was gone crazy, and he didn't care how he went up or hit the ground or even if he broke his own neck so long as he could loosen up that grinning rider and scatter him in the dirt.

"As cow foreman of this outfit, I've seen many a horse buck and many a good cowboy ride. I've seen so many and got so used to it that came a time when I wouldn't even turn my head to see the performance. It was only part of the work; but if I lived to be five hundred I'd never forget what I seen that morning with Dave and the big grey.

No rider had ever been able to make fun of him that way before.

"It was that horse's heart and life *not* to be rode; every muscle along his backbone was against the feel of saddle leather, and many is the time (as we heard later) he throwed both saddle and rider and made 'em hit the ground together. He was an outlaw natural and his pride was on keeping his back clean of any human that tried to set there. His ambition was to kick at 'em as they fell off and step on 'em as they measured their length on mother earth.

"He'd had good luck, and his head was up and mighty confident when he first was run in our corrals, but he hadn't met Dave then and he still had that feeling that he could throw any rider faster than they could climb him.

"So as I was watching that horse that morning I caught myself feeling kinda sorry for the ornery son-of-a-gun. I could see how he was hurt by at last running up against a rider he couldn't shake. And worse yet, that rider was making fun of him.

"But the hardest was still to come; the big gray was bringing in some of his fancy twists, saddle leather was a popping and a machine gun couldn't of kept time for the speed that pony was using in hitting the ground. I was standing inside the log stable which made part of the corral and looking thru one of the windows, and do you know by God I'd even feel that solid log stable shake, so hard did that horse land each jump.

"It was along about when the big gray was doing his best work when I seen Dave do something that sure took my breath away for a spell. That daggone fool leaned down on one side of the saddle, his face came right down alongside the horse's head and looked like he was whispering something in his ear; then he straightened up again, one of his hands went in the air, and in that hand he was holding the hackamore.

"The big gray's head was free, not a string on it; he had more chance to buck than ever before, and that rider a-setting up there was calling him on to do his best. . . . Right then I think something snapped in that bronc's heart strings; that last was too much.

"He quit; legs wide apart he stood there, while Dave sat on him and rolled a smoke. Dave was serious now and pretty soon his hand was running along the gray's mane untangling it some as it went, and then he says to him, 'Never mind, big horse, you sure can buck just the same.' He petted him along the neck a couple of times and climbed off — the horse never moved.

"I think I've told you that I've never seen Dave pet a horse, but I take it back — he did it *that once*.

"Well sir, you wouldn't believe it if you'd seen them horses when Dave started on 'em, but in three months he had 'em all to behaving so as you could do anything with 'em; none of 'em had any buck left — that was wore out of their system by Dave letting 'em have all they wanted of it and a little more. They got so they just naturally hated to buck.

"The big gray? Why, he never bucked since that morning I was telling you of, and he never fought no more either. Instead of that he got to be real attached to Dave and Dave had took such a strong liking for him that he decided to keep him for a 'snubbing' horse and use him to break colts to lead with. Dave often remarked that was one of the best horses he'd ever rode.

"But there's no end of telling what Dave could do and has done with a horse or what a rider he was. It was natural talent with him, and I know that if he'd been born and raised where there's no horses he'd a been a sure and bad failure at anything he'd ever undertook.

"Many is the time when he used to leave me flat and disappear just on account of him hearing about some horse that couldn't be rode. It didn't matter to him whether that horse was in this state or in the next, he'd just up and go; and he'd always come back with a smile.

"Yep! he got real popular that way, and sometimes somebody would even send him a ticket and a request for him to appear at some 'doings' and all they'd have to say to be sure of him being there would be that they had a horse for him nobody in that territory could set — Dave was sure to be present.

"There's not so many riders that can go to any cow or horse outfit with the feeling for sure that they can ride anything that's pointed out to 'em, and as long as I've been with this outfit no strange cowboy has ever come up to me with the remark that they could. It's a wise remark *not* to make and nobody but a greenhorn would pass it; but if there is one man entitled to pass such a remark I don't think there's any what can live up to it like Dave Simmons.

"I know that feller has enjoyed the feeling that he could ride any horse at any time longer than any cowboy I've ever knowed. He could walk in a corral full of ornery outlaws and feel that none of 'em could shake him off, and better than that, he knowed he could ride the worse one in the bunch and laugh at him while that one would near bust hisself a-trying to get him down.

"He was a top rider at eighteen and still one at thirty, which as every bronc rider knows is a mighty long time to ride rough ones; but Dave seemed past human that way. He wasn't a big man, either; never weighed over a hundred and fifty. But he was pretty tall and wiry and the way he could handle himself around a mean horse would make a cougar seem kinda awkward, he done it all so easy. No matter what move a horse made it looked like Dave was always ready for it, and you know, stranger, that a mean horse is never slow in his movements that way, and you also know that them movements come fast and with no thinking spell between.

"There was no main strength and awkwardness with Dave; his was all skill, balance, quick thinking and quick acting; still he never seemed to hurry, either. Everything a horse done seemed to come his way, and

Dave was still in the game at thirty, which is when most of us are ready to quit the rough ones and start looking for the gentler kind.

the more a horse did do the more he was interested. The son-of-a-gun sure enjoyed action!

"Dave was still in the game at thirty, which is about when most of us are ready to quit the rough ones and start looking for the gentler kind. But that wasn't the way with him. He kept right at them rough ones and it aint that he always got away without a scratch either. No, sir; he'd got in many close arguments with the hundreds of different horses he'd rode.

"And as we all know, few mean horses play square; hardly any are what you'd call honest, and sooner or later they get their man. Many will buck out a ways and then throw (not fall) themselves over backwards; others will go up in the air and let their feet go out from under 'em and turn a somerset; sometimes two or three, before they stop rolling. A man ain't got much chance there.

"Then there's these stampeders that take a man thru some awful places. Barb wire, cut banks, hundred-foot cliffs, heavy timber and all is just the same to them. A day of that would put ten years of the prize-fighting game in the kindergarten.

"Them ponies' hoofs are not padded either, and I'd sure like to carry the punch that's back of them hoofs, not mentioning the lightning speed that's with 'em. Even Dave got a wee bit too close to one of them hoofs one time. That was a little while before he quit riding — anyway he layed in the hospital with a broken jaw for quite a spell, and when he come out he was packing a full set of false teeth. A ten-dollar horse had done the damage.

"A while before that another pony had wrapped one of his front legs around Dave's neck and kinked it. He was unconscious when we found him and stayed that way for a few hours. But the next day Dave was out on that same horse and roping bulls with him. Dave couldn't look over his shoulder for a month afterwards.

"I wont mention the bones that's been broke in his body nor how he's all twisted up inside nor how it all happened; that'd make a big book and maybe too close to real life to make good reading. But right now that old boy is packing a silver tube that's running from his knee to his ankle. That leg had been broke so often it was past mending.

"Yessir! Old Dave has sure been through the mill, and you'll say he looks it when you see him. But things wouldn't maybe been quite so hard on him if he hadn't hunted around and looked for a horse he *couldn't* ride. You and me and all cowboys have seen men like Dave; even some of us may've been like him, but for myself I don't care to take that much credit.

"And as I was saying, Dave might of got along better if he hadn't been always looking for a horse he couldn't ride. For fifteen years he tried to find one. Maybe it was just to see if there was such a horse, but anyway he kept a-hunting. Of course, in that time he did run acrost some that made things interesting for him; and a few — mighty few — throwed him. But it wasn't done on the square, and when Dave would climb on 'em again he just made fools out of 'em.

"Then one day we run in a bunch of horses right off our own range. In the bunch was a big brown gelding and a few other colts that Dave was going to keep to break. It was just like Dave to pick on the worse horse first, and the brown gelding seemed about *it*.

"He frontfooted him, throwed him, and I helped slip the hackamore on his head. Dave tied up one foot as I held the horse down, and when that's done we let him up.

"Nothing seemed out of the ordinary with that horse till Dave eased his saddle onto him, and then it struck me right between the eyes, that horse wasn't acting natural. He didn't fight enough and seemed altogether too cool. But what struck me most was them sunk eyes of his. You couldn't tell by looking at 'em what was going on between his ears, and them ears of his drawed my

Some will go up in the air and let their feet go out from under 'em as they come down, and turn a somerset; sometimes two or three, before they stop rolling. A man ain't got much chance there.

attention too. They stuck straight out from both sides of his head and moved neither back or forth; they seemed dead, the same as his eyes. But somehow I didn't want to think just what that combination of ears and eyes and brains was hatching out between 'em just then.

"That horse gave me a hunch that the end of something had come and I come pretty near telling Dave to turn him loose; but before I could think of an excuse the foot rope was off and Dave was on him.

"The big brown just stood in his tracks and shivered for a minute kinda like feeling if his muscles was all answering, and then Dave stirs him by the flat of his hand on his neck. It was just like putting a flame to a keg of powder, and hell broke loose right there.

"I seen Dave get loosened from the first jump, and that never happened before. I didn't want to look no more but somehow I just had to stand there and watch. I couldn't follow the action of that horse, it was too fast, high and crooked, and wicked. His front legs would bend back to a half circle so hard he hit the ground, and his hoofs would sink to the hair in a ground that'd been tamped for years by thousands of other hoofs.

"The saddle on his back was twisting and turning like it was on a pivot, and sometimes even stand straight up on end, the cantle toward the skies.

"By some miracle, Dave was staying there and riding, and he *sure* had to be *riding* to be there, let me tell you; but pretty soon my throat began to get dry, old Dave was loosening up more and more every jump, the saddle was

Their hoofs are not padded and a day of this would put ten years of the prizefighting game in the kindergarten.

steady getting away from him; but the old boy was still a-riding as though he was sure of his seat. His left hand was on the hackamore rope and his right was up in the air and in fanning motion the same as he'd always done. But there was no grin on his face, and believe me, stranger, you don't know how it hit me or what it meant to see that grin fade away.

"Then the end came; the big brown gelding made a leap in the air and for height it broke the record. Then he just seemed to float around up there for a second, both hind feet shot out in a kick that seemed to make the saddle horn and cantle touch, and when he hit the ground he was facing the opposite direction from where he started up. That horse bucked right out from under Dave and left him in the air to come down by himself.

"Well sir, from that day on it was sure some pitiful to watch Dave. None of the boys felt like or wanted to kid him and all was carrying a long face for quite a spell. Riding had been Dave's life and ambition; he done a mighty good job of it and lasted longer than the average, but he'd forgot that a human can stand just so much of that and no more, and he couldn't see why his body had to give out on him when his brain 'was just beginning to function good,' as he'd put it.

"And every day afterward as I'd see Dave going from the bunk house to the corrals it'd come to me how the tables had turned on him. I remembered that time some ten years back when he took the bucking out of that big gray; how he'd near broke the pony's heart when he just

*Both hind feet shot out in a kick that seemed to make the
saddle horn and cantle touch.*

laughed at him and rode him easy and let him buck to his heart's content. That pony had throwed many riders and never been laughed at before that way; it was his pride not to be rode, but Dave took that pride away and made a good saddle horse out of him.

"And now a big brown horse had done the same thing to Dave. It was Dave's pride not to be throwed and he had got to thinking no living horse could do it, till he met that gelding. That gelding maybe couldn't buck much harder than the gray, but then Dave was past being the same rider. Too many rough ponies of that kind had jarred the life out of him and put him in the discard.

"That was bound to come some time, and I was kinda thankful that big brown horse done such an honest job of it. Dave tried him often, and that pony gave him all the chance he wanted and stood still till he was well set. But when Dave would let him know he was ready that pony sure transformed hisself into a full-grown hurricane.

"There was time when as Dave kept a-trying where he showed indications that he was going to stick to the finish; but always when the dust cleared and settled he'd find himself on the ground and getting dirt out of his ears. The brown horse would be to one side all quiet and sort of challenging for him to try again.

"And Dave would try again; he'd try him every day. But every time that pony bucked a little harder, if that was possible; — that horse was fast learning the tricks of the trade while poor old Dave was fast going downhill at it.

"But it was no disgrace getting bucked off that horse, and every man that seen him in action, good riders and all, wondered how many jumps *they* could of stayed. None tried to offer to ride him for Dave; they knowed better for two reasons. One was that Dave wanted to ride that horse himself and without no help; the other was that none of 'em felt at all sure they could ride him and a heap more knowed damn well they couldn't.

"So that's the way things stood. As Dave's friend I tried to talk him into letting that pony and all other broncs go to younger fellers, but he wouldn't listen to it and he'd always come back at me with the remark:

"'I can ride as good as I ever could, and I can ride that brown horse, too. You'll see me do it some of these days, and you'll see me fan and laugh at him the same as I used to do with the others.' But he'd never look me in the eye when he'd say that, and somehow I didn't look up much either.

"It was a month or so later when Dave had to be took to the hospital. Past internal injuries had been stirred up by the brown horse and hemorrhages had started. He layed in the building all that winter, and many is the time we wondered if he'd come out straight up or feet first.

"In his delirious spells he'd lean down on the side of the bed, one arm in the air the same as if he was fanning a bronc; his head would near reach the floor and he'd laugh the same as he'd used to laugh in a bucking horse's ear, and tell the brown horse to do his damndest.

"'I'm with you, you son of a sea cook,' he'd holler at him. 'Let's see if you can shake this cowboy off that brown hide of yours.' The nurse would bust in about then and we'd help her straighten him out.

"The superintendent came along to see him with me one day. He's a stern-looking sort of old feller and always struck me hard as stone; but when he seen Dave act up that way I caught him wiping the moisture off his eyes. It may be that he just realized something he'd never thought of before, but anyway, I sure liked him a heap more after that.

"And while we was hoping for the best for Dave that winter we framed up on him and tried to fix things so there'd be no more broncs for him to ride. There was one man in the country we figgered could ride the brown gelding. He wasn't as good a rider as Dave had been in his prime, but we hired him, thinking he could ride the horse and have him broke before Dave came back. But that horse didn't break so easy as all that, and he throwed his man pretty often — too often for that horse to quit his bucking.

"In the meantime, Dave's constitution, which wouldn't say 'die,' was the cause of him coming out before we expected. He rode up to the ranch one day as big as life and straight to the corral where the new rider was finding himself busy with the brown horse, Dave's brown horse.

"Well sir! Me and the superintendent sure got hell for a few minutes, and we tried to explain; but there was no explaining much to Dave right then. We had to wait till that night before he cooled down so we could talk reason with him, and then we had to give conditions before we could bring the argument to a wind-up.

"The conditions was that we let him have the brown horse and let him try him again soon as he was well recuperated. 'And when I ride him,' he says, 'and make a good job of it, I'll quit and never look at another bronc. But I want to quit knowing that I've rode every horse I ever mounted.'

"That settled it. We raised his wages and gave him an easy job keeping tab on the thoroughbred herd up near the foothills. He'd earned all of that, and we was mighty glad to see him accept. He rode away on a gentle horse, the first gentle horse Dave had rode for fifteen years, and he took his brown horse with him on the end of a rope.

"'Some of these fine days,' he says, pointing at the brown gelding as he was leading him away, 'you'll see me ride him in and right up on the front porch of the superintendent's house.'

"That's been two years ago now and Dave aint showed up on the superintendent's porch as yet, not riding the brown horse, anyway. But I know Dave's been trying to ride that horse again. He may not of been trying very often on account that it takes him too long to get over the effects afterwards, but it aint over a month ago when I rode up there and seen the brown horse in the corral, and seen by the way the hair was laying on his back that the saddle had just been pulled off.

"Dave was lying full length on his bunk when I got up to the cabin, and when he heard me coming he straightened up as though he'd been caught rustling. He hee-hawed around for a spell and finally remarked that them thoroughbreds had sure kept him on the jump that morning, how some broke through the fence and all, but nary a word did he say about that brown horse in the corral. He was mighty careful not to.

"And stranger, that's the way things stand now. You know Dave and his feelings and when you get up there humor the old boy. And if you can frame it up so that Dave can ride that brown horse, or else make him quit and be satisfied, you got a good job here for as long as you want it.

"All of us that knows Dave thinks a powerful lot of him, and we know that if his talent had turned to politics instead of broncs he'd been President of the United States and busted the two-term law all to hell."

The foreman got up from his chair, pointed to a bunk and says, "You can unroll your bed in there for the night if you want, and I'll get some of the boys to help you start out with them horses in the morning."

It was a couple of days later and near sundown when I hazed my bunch of broncs into the corral of the camp

Dave was holding down. On the trail over I'd been thinking steady of what the foreman had told me about him, and I was right anxious to see that hombre.

I was unsaddling my horse when glancing through the corral bars I spots him making tracks towards me. I took in all about him and looked for familiar signs, and even though he was like a lot of cowboys I'd seen and knowed I could see he was a plum stranger to me. I'd been hoping him and me had run acrost one another somewheres before.

But as he got closer and put out his paw for me to shake, I felt right then that I wouldn't of gained anything if we had exchanged the "makings" before. With all what the foreman had already told me about Dave and what I could see myself from one squint at him, not mentioning the feel of his handshake, made things mighty easy for me to know that old boy, and I knowed right there that if I'd broke horses in the same corral with him for the past ten years we wouldn't be no more acquainted than we was in that short spell we'd met.

"I heard a considerable about you," he says as a starter, "and I'm mighty glad to notice by the string of broncs you brought here to break that you're going to be with me for quite some time. Bring your pack-horse on up to the house and we'll put your bed inside while we're at it."

That evening and part of the night was mighty well used up with all we had to say. We talked most of what was past and the countries we'd been in, the ponies we'd rode and the times we'd had here and there. Many things

One squint at him and I felt right there that I wouldn't of knowed him any better if we'd broke horses in the same corral for ten years.

was made to happen again by the old box stove that night, and as the time slid by I gradually edged out of the talk and was finding a lot of pleasure in just listening to Dave.

I could see that hombre had sure took bronc riding to heart and as he talked it was plain to see his heart still layed that way. It was hard for him to quit and the two years he'd been away from the rough ponies only left a hankering that was all the stronger.

"You know, Bill," he says, "It's sure been pounded to me a-plenty that it's high time for me to quit, but I still have the craving for setting on the kinky ponies and hearin' 'em snort back at me as I ride 'em out of the corral. These I'm riding now don't kick at my spurs like them others use to and I kinda miss that; and another thing, it sure worries me to feel that I'm now a 'has-been.'

"But I know it's no use, and that's been proved to me often. It took only one horse to prove it, but that pony sure persuades strong and without a doubt. He took all the conceit out of me and done it easy. That was a hard jolt and not at all gradual and that's one reason why I want to ride that horse. I'm going to ride him, too, and when I have him broke into a good saddle horse why then I'll be ready to quit, not before."

I could see there was no use arguing with Dave on that subject. All I could do was to try and help him win out that once. But he wouldn't stand for no help and every time he'd run in the big gelding and try his hand once more at setting him to a finish, that day would be sure to wind up mighty disappointing for both Dave and me.

"But I'll get him next time," he'd always say.

As the days and weeks wore on and once in a while Dave would try again with no better result, I kept a-trying to figger some way so as that brown hunk of horse meanness would sort of tame down and let Dave stay on for once. There was some ways that it could be done, but I didn't want to think of the consequences if I'd ever got caught trying 'em. It would spoil everything for Dave, for I knowed he wanted to ride that horse as he was and wouldn't want anybody to interfere that way.

Every minute of spare time he had he'd be in the corral watching me ride my colts, and from the way he took in everything I understood why I was sent there to do the horse breaking. The owners of the outfit, respecting Dave's feelings, didn't want him to break away too soon from what he'd been raised to seeing and doing and made a success at. They figgered it'd help some even if he couldn't mix in no more to just watch some other feller do it and let things wear off gradual that way. Not many outfits, I thought, would do that for their riders that got "stove-up" on their range, riding their horses.

I climbed off a pretty "oily" bronc one day and thought I'd rode him slick enough considering the crooked work he put in his bucking. Dave had been watching the performance as usual, and when I walked over to where he was standing by the snubbing post to get my hobbles he says to me:

"You know, Bill, there was a time when I could ride like you rode just now."

I noticed his voice was trembling as he spoke, and I looked over his way. His hat kept me from seeing his face, but the way his hands was shaking as he tried to roll a cigarette told me plain which way his thoughts were running.

A few days later Dave was finding himself busy trying to keep some of his thoroughbred stock under fence; a few was bound to be out and straying away every day when Dave would have to track 'em down and bring 'em back to the big fields. I'd be by my lonesome for the biggest part of the day, and that's what I wanted.

Soon as Dave would disappear and was gone long enough so I was sure of him not turning back on account of forgetting something, I'd run in the big brown gelding, saddle him up and mount him on the fly. We'd go around and around and pretty soon I'd have the feeling that we'd run up in a stone wall. He'd break in two, and from then on is when I had to ride.

He was a rough pony, that boy, and sometimes would suggest mighty strong that I should grab the "nubbin," but somehow I kept my hands free from leather and managed to sideswipe him along the ears with my hat every once in a while. He never liked that, and as I'd hand him that kind of medicine every time I rode him he soon learned that the only way to keep me from doing it was to carry his head up where it belonged and trot around the corral peaceable.

But I didn't want to take all the bucking out of him. I had to leave some for Dave or else that hombre would be sure to see that all wasn't well. So, with a lot of work and hard riding, I finally broke that gelding to ease up on his bucking the minute I hollered at him. He'd took a lot of persuading to show that I could *make* him do that, but before I turned him loose one day I had him where all I had to do was to let out my war whoop and his head would come up like it'd been shot out of the earth by a cannon. I had him ready.

I wanted Dave to put in his work on that gelding the next morning, while I had him under my thumb, and Dave wasn't slow in taking up my hint that it was about time for him to try again. I run the brown horse in with the other colts I was breaking; Dave roped him, saddled him, and was pulling down his hat and pulling up his chaps ready to straddle him when he turned to me and says:

"This pony don't seem quite so spooky to-day."

"Maybe he aint feeling well," I says, as I picks up my rope right quick and make tracks away from there.

I stopped at a safe distance from any more such remarks and watched him ease up in the saddle and get well set. He was mighty serious as he done that, and I could see what he expected was the same as he'd always got in trying to ride that horse. Then the big gelding went into action.

Gradually his jumps got higher and crookeder and each time he hit the ground harder, till I got a glance at Dave getting loosened up again, and I hollered. The horse remembered that holler and come damn near queering things by quitting all at once. I breathed some easier when he went to bucking again; that break in the performance had saved Dave. He'd got his seat back under him once more and then his features lit up into a grin. He was riding him, and daggone it he was even fanning him off and on.

And when the horse would get too rambunctious again I'd just holler out, but not quite so loud as the first time. Finally the doings quieted down, the gelding slowed down to crowhops and then high loping around the corral. Dave was a-setting up there proud as a peacock and grinning from ear to ear.

He was like a kid on Christmas morning when he finally climbed off and went to unsaddling. He was a-jabbering away at me and the gelding and petting him on the neck the while remarking that they'd get along yet. Then he turned on me sudden and asked:

"What t' hell made you holler like that when I was riding?"

I'd been expecting that from him, and my answer was ready.

"That was just my war whoop," I says. "I just can't help but let it out when I see somebody put up a good ride."

But it seemed like he never heard me as I explained, he was thinking of something. Something which showed on his expression as mighty important and sort of cheerful, too, for pretty soon he come out of his trance and says:

"Tomorrow, Bill, I'm going to ride the brown horse right up to the superintendent's house, and right on the front porch. I tole 'em I would do it some day."

Tomorrow came, Dave rode his horse again with the help of my war whoops. Then I opened the corral gate and let 'em go, old Dave a-riding like a cyclone and the brown horse carrying him on.

I sure wished him luck as I watched him top a ridge and disappear on the other side full speed ahead. I knowed what it meant for him to be able to ride up on *that* front porch with *that* brown horse, and somehow as I closed the corral gate I was finding myself hoping that I wouldn't take things so hard when the time came for me to quit the rough ones.

It was my life, too; I enjoyed the feeling that I could ride any horse and I liked them ponies for their orneriness, for the fight they'd put up and how interesting they made things, till they'd finally give in and do as *I* wanted 'em to.

I picked up my rope, packed my saddle by the snubbing post and went to work. There was ten head of broncs in the corral. It was my day's work to "uncork" all of 'em and give 'em each a spell under me and my saddle.

I was saddling up a second horse when I noticed a dust coming back over the same ridge Dave had took. A horse with a saddle on him was making that dust. Stirrups was flapping on each side and nobody was on him. Then I recognized the horse. It was the big brown gelding.

In another second I was on my bronc and headed from where the brown gelding had come. The bronc under me wanted to slow down some and juggle me a little, but I wouldn't give him time. He'd have to do it on the run.

I run onto Dave a mile or so from the corrals. He was all doubled up and leaning against a sage brush and I don't think he knowed I was there till I was near on top of him.

"Are you hurt, Dave?" I asks.

"No, just got the wind knocked out of me a little," he says. "I'll be all right in a minute."

But I knowed the symptoms, and knowed it'd take him quite a few days to recuperate. Dave was mighty quiet the rest of that day. He was doing a lot of thinking and would only grin sort of foolish when I'd look at him. It was after supper before he loosened up and decided to tell how it happened.

"I never was so surprised in my life as when that horse throwed me," he says. "He had me loosened up from the first jump, and I don't remember anything about the second."

Then he's quiet again for a spell, and finally he goes on:

"I guess it's no use, Bill. I've got to quit — I've met him."

"Met who?" I asks.

"My Waterloo," he answers, grinning.